W9-AGR-308

The lives of fifty-nine passengers and crew members on board the plummeting airliner were in the hands of three brave people:

Janet Benson—The blonde, 21-year-old stewardess, who suddenly found that she had to work the controls.

Dr. Baird—"I know nothing about flying. All I know is this. There are people on this plane who will die within a few hours . . ."

George Spencer—Thirteen years ago he had flown single-engine fighter planes. He felt like screaming, "I told you I couldn't do it and you wouldn't listen to me."

RUNWAY ZERO-EIGHT

RUNWAY ZERO-EIGHT

BY ARTHUR HAILEY AND JOHN CASTLE

BANTAM BOOKS
TORONTO · NEW YORK · LONDON

All of the characters in this book are fictitious, and any resemblance to actual persons, living or dead, is purely coincidental.

This low-priced Bantam Book
has been completely reset in a type face
designed for easy reading, and was printed
from new plates. It contains the complete
text of the original hard-cover edition.
NOT ONE WORD HAS BEEN OMITTED.

RUNWAY ZERO-EIGHT
A Bantam Book / published by arrangement with
Doubleday and Company, Inc.

PRINTING HISTORY
Doubleday edition published March 1959
Bantam edition published April 1960
Bantam Pathfinder edition published January 1966
New Bantam edition published July 1969

2nd printing
3rd printing

All rights reserved.
Copyright © 1958 by Arthur Hailey, Ronald Payne and
John Garrod.
This book may not be reproduced in whole or in part, by
mimeograph or any other means, without permission.
For information address: Doubleday and Company, Inc.,
277 Park Avenue, New York, N.Y. 10017.

Published simultaneously in the United States and Canada

Bantam Books are published by Bantam Books, Inc., a subsidiary
of Grosset & Dunlap, Inc. Its trade-mark, consisting of the words
"Bantam Books" and the portrayal of a bantam, is registered in the
United States Patent Office and in other countries. Marca Registrada.
Bantam Books, Inc., 271 Madison Avenue, New York, N.Y. 10016.

PRINTED IN THE UNITED STATES OF AMERICA

Although airlines throughout the world operate on Greenwich Mean Time so far as their crews are concerned, the journey of over 1,500 miles from Winnipeg to Vancouver involves three local time zones: Central Time, Mountain Time, and Pacific Time. This double resetting of the clock each time to put the hands back an hour, would be chronologically confusing in the story which follows. One standard time, therefore, has been assumed throughout.

It is hardly necessary to add that the events, the airlines, and all the persons mentioned are entirely fictitious.

FLIGHT
LOG

ONE

2205—0045

STEADY RAIN slanting through the harsh glare of its headlights, the taxicab swung into the approach to Winnipeg Airport, screeched protestingly round the asphalt curve and, braking hard, came to a spring-shuddering stop outside the bright neons of the reception building. Its one passenger almost leaped out, tossed a couple of bills to the driver, seized an overnight bag and hurried to the swing doors.

Inside, the warmth and lights of the big hall halted him for a moment. With one hand he turned down the collar of his damp topcoat, glanced at the wall clock above him, then half strode, half ran to where the departure desk of Cross-Canada Airlines stood barlike in a corner, deserted now except for the passenger agent checking through a manifest. As the man reached him the agent picked up a small stand microphone on the desk, summoned the man to silence with a lift of his eyebrows, and with measured precision began to speak.

"Flight 98. Flight 98. Direct fleetliner service to Vancouver, with connections for Victoria, Seattle, and Honolulu, leaving immediately through gate four. All passengers for Flight 98 to gate four, please. No smoking till you are in the air."

A group of people rose from the lounge seats, or detached themselves from a bored perusal of the newsstand, and made their way thankfully across the hall. The man in the topcoat opened his mouth to speak but was practically elbowed aside by an elderly woman stuttering in her anxiety.

"Young man," she demanded, "is Flight 63 from Montreal in yet?"

"No, madam," said the passenger agent smoothly. "It's running"—he consulted his list—"approximately thirty-seven minutes late."

"Oh, dear. I've arranged for my niece to be in——"

"Look," said the man in the topcoat urgently, "have you got a seat on Flight 98 for Vancouver?"

The passenger agent shook his head. "Sorry, sir. Not one. Have you checked with Reservations?"

"Didn't have time. Came straight to the airport on the chance of a cancellation." The man slapped the desk in frustration. "You sometimes have one, I know."

"Quite right, sir. But with the big game on in Vancouver tomorrow things are chock full. All our flights are completely booked—I doubt if you'll be able to get out of here before tomorrow afternoon."

The man swore softly, dropped his bag to the floor, and tipped his dripping felt hat to the back of his head. "Of all the lousy deals. I've got to be in Vancouver by tomorrow noon at the latest."

"Don't be so rude," snapped the old lady testily. "I was talking. Now, young man, listen carefully. My niece is bringing with her——"

"Just a moment, madam," cut in the passenger agent. He leaned across the desk and tapped the

2

sleeve of the man with his pencil. "Look, I'm not supposed to tell you this——"

"Yes, what?"

"Well, really!" exploded the old lady.

"There's a charter flight in from Toronto. They're going out to the coast for this game. I believe they were a few seats light when they came in. Perhaps you could grab one of those."

"That's great," exclaimed the man in the topcoat, picking up his bag again. "Do you think there's a chance?"

"No harm in trying."

"Where do I ask then? Who's the guy to see?"

The agent grinned and waved across the hall. "Right over there. The Maple Leaf Air Charter. But mind, I didn't say a thing."

"This is scandalous!" stormed the old lady. "I'll have you know that my niece——"

"Thanks a lot," said the man. He walked briskly over to a smaller desk displaying the fascia board of the air charter company, behind which another agent, this time in a dark lounge suit instead of the smart uniform of the Cross-Canada Airlines, sat busily writing. He looked up as the man arrived, pencil poised, all attention. "Sir?"

"I wonder, can you help me? Have you by any chance a seat left on a flight to Vancouver?"

"Vancouver. I'll see." The pencil checked rapidly down a passenger list. Then: "Uh-huh, just one. Flight's leaving straight away, though; it's overdue as it is."

"That's fine, fine. Can I have that seat, please?"

The agent reached for a ticket stub. "Name, sir?"

"George Spencer." It was entered quickly, with the flight details.

"That's sixty-five dollars for the one-way trip, sir. Thank you; glad to be of service. Any bags, sir?"

"Only one. I'll keep it with me."

In a moment the bag was weighed and labelled.

"Here you are then, sir. The ticket is your boarding pass. Go to gate three and ask for Flight 714. Please hurry, sir: the plane's about to leave."

Spencer nodded, turned away to give a thumbs-up to the Cross-Canada desk, where the passenger agent grimaced in acknowledgment over the old lady's shoulder, and hurried to the departure gate. Outside, the chill night air pulsated with the whine of aero engines; as with any busy airport after dark, all seemed to be in confusion but was in fact part of a strictly regulated, unvarying pattern. A commissionaire directed him across the floodlit apron, gleaming in the rain, to a waiting aircraft whose fuselage seemed a shining silver dart in the light of the overhead arc lamps. Already men were preparing to disengage the passenger ramp. Bounding across the intervening puddles, Spencer reached them, handed over the detachable half of his ticket, and ran lightly up the steps, a gust of errant wind plucking at his hat. He ducked into the aircraft and stood there fighting to regain his breath. He was joined shortly by a stewardess, a mackintosh draped round her, who smiled and made fast the door. As she did, he felt the motors start.

"Out of condition, I guess," he said apologetically.

"Good evening, sir. Pleased to have you aboard."

"I was lucky to make it."

"There's a seat for'ard," said the girl.

4

Spencer slipped out of his coat, took off his hat, and walked along the aisle till he came to the vacant seat. He bundled his coat with some difficulty into an empty spot on the luggage rack, remarking, "They never seem to make these things big enough," to the neighboring passenger who sat looking up at him, disposed of his bag under the seat, and then sank gratefully down on to the soft cushions.

"Good evening," came the stewardess' sprightly voice over the public address system. "The Maple Leaf Air Charter Company welcomes aboard its new passengers to Flight 714. We hope you will enjoy your flight. Please fasten your safety belts. We shall be taking off in a few moments."

As Spencer fumbled with his catch, the man next to him grunted, "That's a pretty sobering sentence. Don't often see it," and nodded down to a small notice on the back of the seat in front reading *Your lifebelt is under the seat*.

Spencer laughed. "*I'd* certainly have been sunk if I hadn't caught this bus," he said.

"Oh? Pretty keen fan, eh?"

"Fan?" Spencer remembered that this was a charter flight for a ball game. "Er—no," he said hastily. "I hadn't given the game a thought. I hate to admit it but I'm rushing off to Vancouver to keep a business appointment. I'd sure like to see that game, but it's out of the question, I'm afraid."

His companion lowered his voice as conspiratorially as was possible against the rising note of the engines. "I shouldn't say that too loudly, if I were you. This plane is crammed with squareheads who are going to Vancouver with one purpose only— and that's to root like hell for their boys and to

5

roar damnation and defiance at the enemy. They're quite likely to do you harm if you use such a light tone about it."

Spencer chuckled again and leaned out from his seat to look round the crowded cabin. There was evidence in plenty of a typical, noisy, roistering but good-natured party of sports fans traveling with the one objective of vanquishing the opposing team and triumphing with their own. To Spencer's immediate right sat a man and his wife, their noses buried in the lurid pages of sports magazines. Behind them, four supporters were pouring rye into paper tumblers and preparing to make a night of it by arguing the respective merits of various players; a snatch of their conversation came over to him like a breath of the field itself. "Haggerty? *Haggerty?* Don't give me that stuff. He's not in the same league as the Thunderbolt. Now *there's* a man for you, if you like. . . ." Behind the slightly alcoholic foursome were other obvious team supporters wearing favors with the colors of their team; mostly big, red-faced men intent on playing the game that lay ahead in Vancouver before it took place.

Spencer turned to the man beside him. Trained to observe detail, he noted the quiet suit, of good cut originally but now well-crumpled, the tie that didn't match, the lined face and graying hair, the indefinable impression of confidence and authority. A face of character, Spencer decided. Behind it the blue lights of the perimeter track had begun to slide past as the aircraft rolled forward.

"I sound like a heretic," said Spencer conversationally, "but I must confess that I'm on my way to the coast on a sales trip, and a mighty important one at that."

His companion showed a polite interest. "What do you sell?" he inquired.

"Trucks. Lots of trucks."

"Trucks, eh? I thought they were sold by dealers."

"So they are. I get called for when a deal is cooking that involves maybe thirty to a hundred trucks. The local salesmen don't like me too well because they say I'm the sharpshooter from head office with the special prices. Selling has its little problems, all right. Still, it's a reasonable living." Spencer rummaged for his cigarettes, then stopped himself. "Heck, I shouldn't be smoking. We're not in the air yet, are we?"

"If we are, we're flying pretty low. And at nil knots."

"Just as well, then." Spencer stretched his legs in front of him. "Man, I'm tired. It's been one of those goofy days that send you up the wall. Know what I mean?"

"I think so."

"First this bird decides he likes a competitor's trucks better after all. Then, when I've sold him the deal and figure I can close the order over supper tonight and be back with my wife and kids by tomorrow night, I get a wire telling me to drop everything and be in Vancouver by lunchtime tomorrow. A big contract is going off the rails there and fast. So Buster must go in and save the day." Spencer sighed, then sat upright in mock earnestness. "Hey, if you want forty or fifty trucks today I can give you a good discount. Feel like running a fleet?"

7

The man beside him laughed. "Sorry, no. I couldn't use that many, I'm afraid. A bit outside my usual line of work."

"What line of work is that?" asked Spencer.

"Medicine."

"A doctor, eh?"

"Yes, a doctor. And therefore of no use to you in the disposal of trucks, I'm afraid. I couldn't afford to buy one, let alone forty. Football is the only extravagance I can allow myself, and for that I'd travel anywhere, provided I could find the time. Hence my trip tonight."

Leaning back on the headrest of his seat, Spencer said, "Glad to have you around, Doctor. If I can't sleep you can prescribe me a sedative."

As he spoke the engines thundered to full power, the whole aircraft vibrating as it strained against the wheel brakes.

The doctor put his mouth to Spencer's ear and bellowed, "A sedative would be no good in this racket. I never could understand why they have to make all this noise before take-off."

Spencer nodded; then, when after a few seconds the roar had subsided sufficiently for him to make himself heard without much trouble, he said, "It's the usual run-up for the engines. It's always done before the plane actually starts its take-off. Each engine has two magnetos, in case one packs in during flight, and in the run-up each engine in turn is opened to full throttle and each of the mags tested separately. When the pilot has satisfied himself that they are running okay he takes off, but not before. Airlines have to be fussy that way, thank goodness."

"You sound as though you knew a lot about it."

"Not really. I used to fly fighters in the war but I'm pretty rusty now. Reckon I've forgotten most of it."

"Here we go," commented the doctor as the engine roar took on a deeper note. A powerful thrust in the backs of their seats told them the aircraft was gathering speed on the runway; almost immediately a slight lurch indicated that they were airborne and the engines settled back to a steady hum. Still climbing, the aircraft banked steeply and Spencer watched the receding airport lights as they rose steadily over the wingtip.

"You may unfasten your safety belts," announced the public address. "Smoke if you wish."

"Never sorry when that bit's over," grunted the doctor, releasing his catch and accepting a cigarette. "Thanks. By the way, I'm Baird, Bruno Baird."

"Glad to know you, Doc. I'm Spencer, plain George Spencer, of the Fulbright Motor Company."

For some time the two men lapsed into silence, absently watching their cigarette smoke rise slowly in the cabin until it was caught by the air-conditioning stream and sucked away. Spencer's thoughts were somber. There would have to be some kind of a showdown when he got back to head office, he decided. Although he had explained the position on the telephone to the local Winnipeg man before calling a taxi for the airport, that order would take some holding on to now. It would have to be a big show in Vancouver to justify this snafu. It might be a good idea to use the whole thing as a lever for a pay raise when he got back. Or better yet, promotion. As a manager in the dealer sales division, which the old man had often mentioned but never got around to, Mary and he, Bobsie and little Kit, could get out of the house they had and move up Parkway Heights. Or pay off the bills—the new water tank, school fees, installments on the Olds and the deep freeze, hospital charges for Mary's last pregnancy. Not both, Spencer reflected broodingly; not both, even on manager's pay.

Dr. Baird, trying to decide whether to go to sleep or to take this excellent opportunity to catch up on the airmail edition of the *B.M.J.*, in fact did neither and found himself instead thinking about the small-town surgery he had abandoned for a couple of days. Wonder how Evans will cope, he thought. Promising fellow, but absurdly young. Hope to goodness he remembers that Mrs. Lowrie has ordinary mist. expect. and not the patent medicine fiddle-me-rees she's always agitating for. Still Doris would keep young Evans on the right track; doctors' wives were wonderful like that. Had to be, by jiminy. That was a thing Lewis would have to learn in due time: to find the right woman. The doctor dozed a little and his cigarette burnt his fingers, promptly waking him up.

The couple in the seats across the aisle were still engrossed in their sports papers. To describe Joe Greer was to describe Hazel Greer: a pair who would be hard to imagine. Both had the rosy skin and the keen, clear eyes of the open air, both bent over the closely printed sheets as if the secrets of the universe were there displayed. "Barley sugar?" asked Joe when the airline tray came around. "Uh-huh," replied Hazel. Then, munching steadily, down again went the two brown heads of hair.

The four in the seats behind were starting their third paper-enclosed round of rye. Three were of the usual type: beefy, argumentative, aggressive, out to enjoy themselves with all the customary restraints cast aside for two memorable days. The fourth was a short, thin, lean-featured man of lugubrious expression and indeterminate age who spoke with a full, round Lancashire accent. " 'Ere's t'Lions t'morrer," he called, raising his paper cup in yet another toast to their heroes. His friends acknowledged the rubric solemnly. One of them, his coat lapel displaying a badge which appeared to depict a mangy alley cat in rampant mood but presumably represented the king of beasts himself, passed round his cigarette case and remarked, not for the first time, "Never thought we'd make it, though. When we had to wait at Toronto with that fog around, I said to myself, 'Andy,' I said, 'this is one bit of hell-raising you're going to have to miss.' Still, we're only a few hours late for all that and we can always sleep on the plane."

"Not before we eat, though, I hope," said one of the others. "I'm starving. When do they bring round the grub?"

"Should be along soon, I reckon. They usually serve dinner about eight, but everything's been pu? behind with that holdup."

"Never mind. 'Ave a drink while you wait, suggested the Lancashire man, who rejoiced in th nickname of 'Otpot, holding out the bottle of rye.

"Go easy, boy. We haven't got too much."

"Ah, there's plenty more where this came from. Come on, now. It'll help you sleep."

The rest of the fifty-six passengers, who included three or four women, were reading or talking, all

11

looking forward to the big game and excited to be on the last leg of their transcontinental journey. From the port windows could be seen the twinkling blue and yellow lights of the last suburbs of Winnipeg, before they were swallowed in cloud as the aircraft climbed.

In the tiny but well-appointed galley Stewardess Janet Benson prepared for dinner, a belated meal that she should have served over two hours earlier. The mirror over the glassware cabinet reflected the exhilaration she always felt at the beginning of a flight, an exuberance which she was thankful to hide in the privacy of her own quarters. Taking from built-in cupboards the necessary napkins and cutlery, Janet hummed contentedly to herself. Waitressing was the least attractive part of a stewardess' duties, and Janet knew that she was in for a very exhausting hour catering for the stomachs of a planeload of hungry people, but nevertheless she felt confident and happy. Many of her flying colleagues, if they could have watched the swing of r blond hair from beneath her airline cap and movements of her trim body as she busied elf efficiently about the galley, would have given ppreciative sucking-in of breath and echoed dence. At twenty-one, Janet was just tast- d finding it good.

e l on the flight deck, the only sound was the steady drone and throb of the engines. Both pilots sat perfectly still except for an occasional leg or arm movement, their faces faintly illuminated in the glow of light from the myriad dials on the instrument panels. From the earphones half covering their ears came the sudden crackle of conversation between another aircraft and the ground. Round their necks hung small boom microphones.

Captain Dunning stretched himself in his seat, flexing his muscles and blew out through the luxuriant growth of his mustache in an unconscious mannerism that his crew knew well. He looked older than his thirty-one years.

"How are the cylinder head temperatures on Number 3 engine, Pete?" he asked, his eyes flickering momentarily to the first officer.

Pete stirred and glanced at the panel. "Okay now, skip. I had it checked at Winnipeg but they couldn't find anything wrong. Seems to have righted itself. It's not heating up now."

"Good." Dun peered ahead at the night sky. A thin moon shone bleakly down on the banks of cloud. Shredded wisps of cotton wool lazily approached, to suddenly whisk by; or occasionally the ship would plunge into a tumble of gray-white cloud, to break free in a second or two like a spaniel leaving the water and shaking itself free of the clinging drops. "With a bit of luck it'll be a clear run through," he commented. "The met report was reasonable for a change. Not often you keep to the original flight plan on this joyride."

"You said it," agreed the first officer. "In a month or so's time it'll be a very different story."

The aircraft began to bump and roll a little as she hit a succession of thermal currents and for a few minutes the captain concentrated on correcting her trim. Then he remarked, "Are you planning to take in this ball game in Vancouver, if there's time to rest up first?"

The first officer hesitated before answering. "I

don't know yet," he answered. "I'll see how it works out."

The captain looked sharply at him. "What d'you mean? See how what works out? If you've got your eyes on Janet, you can take them off again. She's too young to come under the corrupting influence of a young Casanova like you."

Few people looked less deserving of this description than the fresh-faced, thoughtful-eyed first officer, still in his twenties. "Go easy, skipper," he protested, coloring. "I never corrupted anyone in my life."

"Jeepers, that's a likely story. Well, don't aim to start with Janet." The captain grinned. "Half the airlines personnel of Canada regard it as a permanent assignment to try to make her. Don't make life hard for yourself, you chump."

Twelve feet away from them, on the other side of a sliding door, the subject of their conversation was collecting orders for the evening meal.

"Would you like dinner now, sir?" she asked quietly, bending forward with a smile.

"Eh? What's that? Oh, yes please." Baird slipped back into the present and nudged Spencer who was practically asleep. "Wake up, there. Want some dinner?"

Spencer yawned and gathered himself together. "Dinner? I sure do. You're late, miss, aren't you? I thought I'd missed it long ago."

"We were held up in Toronto, sir, and haven't served dinner yet," said Janet Benson. "What would you like? We've lamb chop or grilled salmon."

"Er—yes, please."

14

Janet's smile tightened a little. "Which, sir?" she asked patiently.

Spencer came fully awake. "Oh, yes—I'm sorry, miss. I'll have lamb."

"Me too," said Baird.

Back in the galley, Janet was fully occupied for the next half hour in preparing and serving meals. Eventually everyone who felt like eating had been served with a main course and she was free to pick up the telephone in the galley and press the intercom buzzer.

"Flight deck," came the voice of Pete.

"I'm finally serving dinner," said Janet. "Better late than never. What'll it be—lamp chop or grilled salmon?"

"Hold it." She could hear him putting the question to the captain. "Janet, skipper says he'll have the lamb—no, just a sec, he's changed his mind. Is the fish good?"

"Looks okay to me," said Janet chirpily. "Had no complaints."

"Skipper will take salmon, then. Better make it two. Big helpings, mind. We're growing boys."

"All right—double portions as usual. Two fish coming up."

She quickly arranged two trays and took them forward, balancing them with practiced ease against the almost imperceptible movements of the aircraft. Pete had come back to open the sliding door for her and relieved her of one tray. The captain had completed his switchover to automatic pilot and was now halfway through his routine radio check with Control at Winnipeg.

"Height 16,000," he continued, speaking into the tiny microphone held before his mouth on a slender plastic arm. "Course 285 true. Air speed 210 knots. Ground speed 174 knots. ETA Vancouver 05.05 Pacific Standard. Over."

He switched from transmit to receive and there was a clearly audible crackle from his earpiece as the acknowledgment came on the air. "Flight 714. This is Winnipeg Control. Roger. Out."

Dun reached for his log sheet, made an entry, then slid his seat back so that he was well clear of the controls but still within easy reach of them if it were necessary for him to take them over again quickly. Pete was starting to eat, a tray resting on a pillow laid across his knees.

"Shan't be long, skip," he said.

"There's no hurry," replied Dun, stretching his arms above his head as far as they could go in the confined cockpit. "I can wait. Enjoy it. How is the fish, anyway?"

"Not bad," mumbled the first officer, his mouth full. "If there were about three or four times as much it might be a square meal."

The captain chuckled. "You'd better watch that waistline, Pete." He turned to the stewardess, who was waiting in the shadow behind the seat. "Everything okay at the back, Janet? How are the football fans?"

Janet shrugged. "Very quiet now. That long wait at Toronto must have tired them out. Four of them have been knocking back rye pretty steadily, but there's been no need to speak to them about it. It'll help to keep them quiet. It looks like being a peaceful, easy night—fingers crossed."

Pete raised a quizzical eyebrow. "Uh-huh, young woman. That's the kind of night to watch, when

16

trouble starts to brew. I'll bet someone's getting ready to be sick right now."

"Not yet," said Janet lightly. "But you warn me when *you're* going to fly the ship and I'll get the bags ready."

"Good for you," said the captain. "I'm glad you found out about him."

"How's the weather?" asked Janet.

"Oh—now let's see. General fog east of the mountains, extending nearly as far as Manitoba. There's nothing to bother us up there, though. It should be a smooth ride all the way to the coast."

"Good. Well, keep Junior here off the controls while I serve coffee, won't you?"

She slipped away before Pete could retort, made her way through the passenger deck taking orders for coffee, and within a short while brought a tray up forward to the pilots. Dun had by that time eaten his dinner, and he now drained his coffee with satisfaction. Pete had taken the controls and was intent on the instrument dials as the captain got to his feet.

"Keep her steaming, Pete. I'll just tuck the customers up for the night."

Pete nodded without turning round. "Right, skipper."

The captain followed Janet out into the brightly lit passenger section, blinking, and stopped first at the seats occupied by Spencer and Baird, who handed their trays to the stewardess.

"Good evening," said Dun. "Everything all right?"

Baird looked up. "Why sure, thanks. Very nice meal. We were ready for it, too."

"Yes, I'm sorry it was so late."

17

The doctor waved aside his apology. "Nonsense. You can hardly be blamed if Toronto decides to have a bit of fog. Well," he added, settling himself back in his seat, "I'm going to get my head down for a doze."

"That goes for me as well," said Spencer with a yawn.

"I hope you have a comfortable night," said Dun, switching off their reading lights. "The stewardess will bring you some rugs." He passed on down the aisle, having a few words with each of the passengers in a subdued tone, explaining to some how the seats could be reclined, and describing to others the flight's progress and expected weather conditions.

"Well, it's me for dreamland," said Spencer. "One thing, Doctor—at least you won't be getting any calls tonight."

"How long is it?" murmured Baird drowsily, his eyes closed. "A good seven hours anyway. Better make the most of it. 'Night."

"Goodnight, Doc," grunted Spencer, wriggling the padded headrest into the small of his neck. "Boy, I can sure use some shut-eye."

Blanketed off by thick cloud into a cold, remote world of her own, the aircraft droned steadily on her course. Sixteen thousand feet beneath her lay the prairies of Saskatchewan, silent and sleeping.

Dun had reached the whisky-drinking quartet and politely forbade any further consumption of liquor that night.

"You know," he told them with a reproving grin, "this sort of thing isn't permitted anyway. Just don't let me see any more bottles or you'll have to get out and walk."

18

"Any objection to cards?" inquired one of the party, holding a flask to the nearest light and turning down the corners of his mouth at the small amount of nectar that remained.

"Not in the least," said Dun, "so long as you don't disturb the other passengers."

"Pity the poor captain," said the man from Lancashire. "What's it like—taking a massive job like this through t'night?"

"Routine," said Dun. "Just plain, dull routine."

"Comes to that, every flight is just routine, I s'pose?"

"Well, yes. I guess that's so."

"Until summat happens—eh?"

There was an outburst of chuckles in which Dunning joined before moving on. Only the Lancastrian, through the haze of his evening's drinking, looked temporarily thoughtful at his own words.

TWO

0045—0145

THE CAPTAIN had almost completed his rounds and was enjoying a few moments' relaxed chaffing with one of the passengers, a little man who appeared to have traveled with him before.

"I know it looks a bit like R.C.A.F.," Dun was saying, fingering his great bush of a mustache apologetically, "but I've had it so long I couldn't part with it now—it's an old friend, you know."

"I'll bet it's a wow with the girls," said the little man. "What do they call you—Beaver?"

"Well, no," replied Dun, a suspicion of a grin under his foliage. "We're a pretty highbrow lot on this airline. It's either 'Have yer Dun, then? or, most often, just Dunsinane."

"Just what?" asked the little man.

"Dunsinane," said the captain very deliberately. "Surely you know? Where's your *Macbeth*?"

The little man stared up at him. "Where's my *Macbeth*?" he repeated vacantly. "Hey, what are you giving me?"

The captain had moved on. While he had been speaking his eyes had been fixed on the stewardess, further along the aisle, who was bending over a woman, the palm of her hand on the passenger's forehead. As he approached, the woman, who lay

20

rather than sat in her seat, slumped back against the headrest, suddenly grimaced. Her eyes contracted as if with pain. The captain touched the stewardess lightly on the arm.

"Anything wrong, Miss Benson?" he asked.

Janet straightened. "The lady is feeling a little under the weather, Captain," she said very quietly. "I'll get her some aspirin. Be back in a moment."

Dun took her place and leaned over the woman and the man beside her.

"Sorry to hear that," he said sympathetically. "What seems to be the trouble?"

The woman stared up at him. "I—I don't know," she said in a small voice. "It seemed to hit me all of a sudden. Just a few minutes ago. I feel sick and dizzy and—and there's an awful pain . . . down here." She indicated her stomach. "I'm sorry to be a nuisance—I——"

"Now, now, honey," murmured the man beside her. "Just lay quiet. You'll be better directly." He glanced at the captain. "A touch of airsickness, I guess?"

"I expect so, sir," answered Dun. He looked down thoughtfully at the woman, taking in the perspiration beginning to bead on her pallid forehead, the hair already becoming disarranged, the whiteness of her knuckles as with one hand she gripped the armrest of the seat and with the other held on to her husband. "I'm sorry you don't feel well," he said gently, "but I'm sure the stewardess will be able to help you. Try to relax as much as you can. If it's any comfort I can tell you that it looks like being a calm trip."

He moved aside for Janet.

"Now here we are," said the stewardess, handing

21

down the pills. "Try these." She eased the woman's head forward, to help her take a few sips of water from a glass. "That's fine. Now let's make you a little more comfortable." She tucked in a rug round the woman. "How's that?" The woman nodded gratefully. "I'll be back in a few minutes to see how you're feeling. Don't worry about using the paper bag if you want to. And if you need me quickly just press the bell push by the window."

"Thank you, miss," said the husband. "I'm sure we'll be okay in just a little while." He looked at his wife with a smile, as if to reassure himself. "Try to rest, dear. It'll pass over."

"I hope so," said Dun. "I know how unpleasant these things can be. I hope you very soon feel better, madam, and that you both have a good night."

He passed back down the aisle and waited for Janet in the galley. "Who are they?" he asked when the stewardess returned.

"Mr. and Mrs. Childer—John Childer. She was all right fifteen minutes ago."

"H'm. Well, you'd better let me know if she gets any worse and I'll radio ahead."

Janet looked at him quickly. "Why? What are you thinking?"

"I don't know. I don't like the look of her. Could be air-sickness or just a bilious attack, I suppose—but it seems to have hit her pretty hard." The captain looked faintly worried, his fingers drumming absently on the metal draining board. "Have we a doctor on the passenger list?"

"No one who's entered as a doctor," replied Janet, "but I could ask around."

Dun shook his head. "Don't disturb them now.

22

Most of them are getting down to sleep. Let me know how she is in half an hour or so. The trouble is," he added quietly as he turned to go, "we've got over four hours' flying before we reach the coast."

Making his way to the flight deck, he stopped for a moment to smile down at the sick woman. She attempted to smile back, but a sudden stab of pain closed her eyes and made her arch back against the seat. For a few seconds Dun stood studying her intently. Then he continued forward, closed the door of the flight deck behind him, and slid into his seat. He took off his peaked hat and put on the large earphones and then the boom microphone. Pete was flying manually. Scattered banks of cloud seemed to rush at the forward windows, envelop them momentarily, and then disappear.

"Cumulo-nimbus building up," commented the first officer.

"Getting to the rough stuff, eh?" said Dun.

"Looks like it."

"I'll take it. We'd better try to climb on top. Ask for twenty thousand, will you?"

"Right." Pete depressed a stud on his microphone attachment to transmit. "714 to Regina radio," he called.

"Go ahead, 714," crackled a voice in the earphones.

"We're running into some weather. We'd like clearance for twenty thousand."

"714. Stand by. I'll ask ATC."

"Thanks," said Pete.

The captain peered into the cloudy turbulence ahead. "Better switch on the seat-belt sign, Pete," he suggested, correcting with automatic concentration the tendency of the aircraft to bump and yaw.

23

"Okay." Pete reached for the switch on the overhead panel. There was a brief shudder as the plane freed herself from a wall of cloud, only to plunge almost instantly into another.

"Flight 714," came the voice on the radio. "ATC gives clearance for twenty thousand. Over."

"714," acknowledged Pete. "Thanks and out."

"Let's go," said the captain. The note of the engines took on a deeper intensity as the deck began to tilt and the altimeter needle on the winking instrument panel steadily registered a climb of five hundred feet a minute. The long window wiper swished rhythmically in a broad sweep from side to side.

"Shan't be sorry when we're clear of this muck," remarked the first officer.

Dun didn't answer, his eyes glued on the dials in front of him. Neither of the pilots heard the stewardess enter. She touched the captain on the shoulder.

"Captain," she said urgently, but keeping her voice well under control. "That woman. She's worse already. And I have another passenger sick now—one of the men."

Dun did not turn to her. He stretched up an arm and switched on the landing lights. Ahead of them the sharp beams cut into driving rain and snow. He turned off the lights and began to adjust engine and de-icer switches.

"I can't come right now, Janet," he replied as he worked. "You'd better do as we said and see if you can find a doctor. And make sure all the seat belts are fastened. This may get pretty rough. I'll come as soon as I can."

"Yes, Captain."

Emerging from the flight deck, Janet called out in a voice just loud enough to carry to the rows of passengers, "Fasten your safety belts, please. It may be getting a little bumpy." She leaned over the first two passengers to her right, blinking up at her half-asleep. "Excuse me," she said casually, "but do either of you gentlemen happen to be a doctor?"

The man nearest her shook his head. "Sorry, no," he grunted. "Is there something wrong?"

"No, nothing serious."

An exclamation of pain snapped her to attention. She hurried along the aisle to where the sick Mrs. Childer lay half-cradled in her husband's arms, moaning with eyes closed, and partially doubled over. Janet knelt down swiftly and wiped the glistening sweat from the woman's brow. Childer stared at her, his face creased with anxiety.

"What can we do, miss?" he asked her. "What d'you think it is?"

"Keep her warm," said Janet. "I'm going to see if there's a doctor on board."

"A doctor? I just hope there is. What do we do if there isn't?"

"Don't worry, sir. I'll be back straight away."

Janet got to her feet, looked down briefly at the suffering woman, and moved on to the next seats, repeating her question in a low voice.

"Is someone ill?" she was asked.

"Just feeling unwell. It sometimes happens, flying. I'm sorry to have disturbed you."

A hand clutched at her arm. It was one of the whisky quartet, his face yellow and shining.

"Sorry, miss, to trouble you again. I'm feeling like hell. D'you think I could have a glass of water?"

"Yes, of course. I'm on my way now to get it."

"I never felt like this before." The man lay back and blew out his cheeks. One of his companions stirred, opened his eyes and sat up. "What's with you?" he growled.

"It's my insides," said the sick man. "Feels like they're coming apart." His hands clenched his stomach as another spasm shook him.

Janet shook Spencer gently by the shoulder. He opened one eye, then both. "I'm very sorry to wake you up, sir," she said, "but is anyone here a doctor?"

Spencer gathered himself. "A doctor? No. I guess not, miss." She nodded and made to move on. "Just a moment, though," he stopped her. "I seem to remember—yes, of course he is. This gentleman beside me is a doctor."

"Oh, thank goodness," breathed the stewardess. "Would you wake him, please?"

"Sure." Spencer looked up at her as he nudged the recumbent form next to him. "Someone's ill, huh?"

"Feeling a little unwell," said Janet.

"Come on, Doc, wake up," Spencer said heartily. The doctor shook his head, grunted, then snapped awake. "Seems that you've got your night call after all."

"Are you a doctor, sir?" asked Janet anxiously.

"Yes. Yes, I'm Dr. Baird. Why, what's wrong?"

"We have two passengers who are quite sick. Would you take a look at them, please?"

"Sick? Yes, certainly."

Spencer stood up to let the doctor out. "Where are they?" Baird asked, rubbing his eyes.

"I think you'd better see the woman first, Doctor," said Janet, leading the way and at the same time calling out quietly, "Fasten your seat belts, please," as she passed along.

Mrs. Childer was now as prostrate as the seat allowed. Shivers of pain racked her body. She breathed heavily, with long, shuddering gasps. Her hair was wet with sweat.

Baird stood studying her for a moment. Then he knelt and took her wrist.

"This gentleman is a doctor," said Janet.

"Am I glad to see you, Doctor," Childer said fervently.

The woman opened her eyes. "Doctor ..." She made an effort to speak, her lips trembling.

"Just relax," said Baird, his eyes on his watch. He released her wrist, felt in his jacket and took out a pocket flashlight. "Open your eyes wide," he ordered gently and examined each eye in turn in the bright pencil of light. "Now. Any pain?" The woman nodded. "Where? Here? Or here?" As he palpated her abdomen, she stiffened suddenly, choking back a cry of pain. He replaced the blanket, felt her forehead, then stood up. "Is this lady your wife?" he asked Childer.

"Yes, Doctor."

"Has she complained of anything in addition to the pain?"

"She's been very sick, throwing up everything."

"When did it start?"

"Not long, I guess." Childer looked helplessly at Janet. "It's all come on suddenly."

Baird nodded reflectively. He moved away, taking Janet by the arm and speaking very quietly so as not to be overheard by the nearby passengers who were staring up at them.

"Have you given her anything?" he inquired.

27

"Only aspirin and water," replied Janet. "That reminds me. I promised a glass of water to the man who's sick——"

"Wait," said Baird crisply. His sleepiness had vanished now. He was alert and authoritative. "Where did you learn your nursing?"

Janet colored at his tone. "Why, at the airline training school, but—"

"Never mind. But it's not much use giving aspirin to anyone who is actually vomiting—you'll make 'em worse. Strictly water only."

"I—I'm sorry, Doctor," Janet stammered.

"I think you'd better go to the captain," said Baird. "Please tell him we should land at once. This woman has to be gotten to a hospital. Ask to have an ambulance waiting."

"Do you know what's wrong?"

"I can't make a proper diagnosis here. But it's serious enough to land at the nearest city with hospital facilities. You can tell the captain that."

"Very well, Doctor. While I'm gone, will you take a look at the other sick passenger? He's complaining of the same sickness and pains."

Baird looked at her sharply. "The same pains, you say? Where is he?"

Janet led him forward to where the sick man sat, bent over, retching, supported by his friend in the next seat. Baird crouched down to look at his face.

"I'm a doctor. Will you put your head back, please?" As he made a quick examination, he asked, "What have you had to eat in the last twenty-four hours?"

"Just the usual things," muttered the man, all the strength appearing to have been drained from him. "Breakfast," he said weakly, "bacon and eggs

28

... salad for lunch ... a sandwich at the airport ... then dinner here." A trickle of saliva ran disregarded down his chin. "It's this pain, Doctor. And my eyes."

"What about your eyes?" asked Baird quickly.

"Can't seem to focus. I keep seeing double."

His companion seemed to find it amusing. "That rye has got a real kick, yes sir," he exclaimed.

"Be quiet," said Baird. He rose, to find Janet and the captain standing beside him. "Keep him warm—get more blankets round him," he told Janet. The captain motioned him to follow down to the galley. Immediately they were alone, Baird demanded, "How quickly can we land, Captain?"

"That's the trouble," said Dun briefly. "We can't."

Baird stared at him. "Why?"

"It's the weather. I've just checked by radio. There's low cloud and fog right over the prairies this side of the mountains. Calgary's shut in completely. We'll have to go through to the coast."

Baird thought for a moment. "What about turning back?" he asked.

Dun shook his head, his face taut in the soft glow of the lights. "That's out, too. Winnipeg closed down with fog shortly after we left. Anyway, it'll be quicker now to go on."

Baird grimaced, tapping his finger nail with the tiny flashlight. "How soon do you expect to land?"

"About five A.M., Pacific Time." Dun saw the doctor glance involuntarily at his wrist watch, and added, "We're due to land in three and a half hours from now. These charter aircraft aren't the fastest in the world."

Baird made up his mind. "Then I'll have to do

29

what I can for these people until we arrive at Vancouver. I'll need my bag. Do you think it can be reached? I checked it at Toronto."

"We can try," said the captain. "I hope it's near the top. Let me have your tags, Doctor."

Baird's long fingers probed into his hip pocket and came out with his wallet. From this he took two baggage tickets and handed them to Dun.

"There are two bags, Captain," he said. "It's the smaller one I want. There isn't much equipment in it—just a few things I always carry around. But they'll help."

He had barely finished speaking before the aircraft gave a violent lurch. It sent the two men sprawling to the far wall. There was a loud, persistent buzzing. The captain was on his feet first and sprang to the intercom telephone.

"Captain here," he rapped out. "What's wrong, Pete?"

The voice of the first officer was struggling and painful. "I'm . . . sick . . . come quickly."

"You'd better come with me," said Dun to the doctor and they left the galley rapidly. "Sorry about the bump," Dun remarked affably to the upturned faces as they walked along the aisle. "Just a little turbulence."

As they burst into the flight deck, it was only too apparent that the first officer was very sick; his face a mask of perspiration, he was slumped in his seat, clutching the control column with what was obviously all his strength.

"Get him out of there," directed the captain urgently. Baird and Janet, who had followed the men in, seized the copilot and lifted him out and

30

away from the controls, while Dun slipped into his own seat and took the column in his hands.

"There's a seat at the back of the flight deck, for when we carry a radio operator," he told them. "Put him there."

With an agonizing retch, Pete spewed on to the deck as they helped him to the vacant seat and propped him against the wall. Baird loosened the first officer's collar and tie and tried to make him as comfortable as the conditions would allow. Every few seconds Pete would jackknife in another croaking, straining retch.

"Doctor," called the captain, his voice tense, "what is it? What's happening?"

"I'm not sure," said Baird grimly. "But there's a common denominator to these attacks. There has to be. The most likely thing is food. What was it we had for dinner?"

"The main course was a choice of meat or fish," said Janet. "You probably remember, Doctor—you had——"

"Meat!" cut in Baird. "About—what?—two, three hours ago. What did he have?" He indicated the first officer.

Janet's face began to register alarm. "Fish," she almost whispered.

"Do you remember what the other two passengers had?"

"No—I don't think so——"

"Go back quickly and find out, will you, please?"

The stewardess hurried out, her face pale. Baird knelt beside the first officer who sat swaying with the motion of the aircraft, his eyes closed. "Try to relax," he said quietly. "I'll give you something in a few minutes that'll help the pain. Here." He reached up and pulled down a blanket from a rack. "You'll feel better if you stay warm."

Pete opened his eyes a little and ran his tongue over dry lips. "Are you a doctor?" he asked. Baird nodded. Pete said with a sheepish attempt to smile, "I'm sorry about all this mess. I thought I was going to pass out."

"Don't talk," said Baird. "Try to rest."

"Tell the captain he's sure right about my ham-handed——"

"I said don't talk. Rest and you'll feel better."

Janet returned. "Doctor," she spoke rapidly, hardly able to get the words out quickly enough. "I've checked both those passengers. They both had salmon. There are three others complaining of pains now. Can you come?"

"Of course. But I'll need that bag of mine."

Dun called over his shoulder, "Look, I can't leave here now, Doctor, but I'll see that you get it immediately. Janet, take these tags. Get one of the passengers to help you and dig out the smaller of the doctor's two bags, will you?" Janet took the tags from him and turned to the doctor to speak again, but Dun continued, "I'm going to radio Vancouver and report what's happening. Is there anything you want me to add?"

"Yes," said Baird. "Say we have three serious cases of suspected food poisoning and that there seem to be others developing. You can say we're not sure but we suspect that the poisoning could have been caused by fish served on board. Better ask them to put a ban on all food originating from the same source as ours—at least until we've established the cause of the poisoning for certain."

"I remember now," exclaimed Dun. "That food

32

didn't come from the caterers who usually supply the airlines. Our people had to get it from some other outfit because we were so late getting into Winnipeg."

"Tell them that, Captain," said Baird. "That's what they'll need to know."

"Doctor, *please*," Janet implored him. "I do wish you'd come and see Mrs. Childer. She seems to have collapsed altogether."

Baird stepped to the door. The lines in his face had deepened, but his eyes as he held Janet's with them were steady as a rock.

"See that the passengers are not alarmed," he instructed. "We shall be depending on you a great deal. Now if you'll be good enough to find my bag and bring it to me, I'll be attending to Mrs. Childer." He pushed back the door for her, then stopped her as something occurred to him. "By the way, what did *you* eat for dinner?"

"I had meat," the young stewardess answered him.

"Thank heavens for that, then." Janet smiled and made to go on again, but he gripped her suddenly, very hard, by the arm. "I suppose the captain had meat, too?" He shot the question at her.

She looked up at him, as if at the same time trying both to remember and to grasp the implications of what he had asked.

Then, suddenly, shock and realization flooded into her. She almost fell against him, her eyes dilated with an immense and overpowering fear.

THREE

0145—0220

BRUNO BAIRD regarded the stewardess thoughtfully.
Behind the calm reassurance of his blue-gray eyes
his mind rapidly assessed the situation, weighing
with the habit of years one possibility against another. He released the girl's arm.

"Well, we won't jump to conclusions," he said,
almost to himself. Then, more briskly, "You find
my bag—just as quickly as you can. Before I see
Mrs. Childer I'll have another word with the captain."

He retraced his steps forward. They were now in
level flight, above the turbulence. Over the pilot's
shoulder he could see the cold white brilliance of
the moon, converting the solid carpet of cloud
below them into a seemingly limitless landscape of
snow with here and there what looked for all the
world like a pinnacle of ice thrusting its craggy
outcrop through the surrounding billows. The
effect was dreamlike.

"Captain," he said, leaning over the empty copilot's seat. Dun looked round, his face drawn and
colorless in the moon glare. "Captain, this has to
be fast. There are people very sick back there and
they need attention."

Dun nodded quickly. "Yes, Doctor. What is it?"

"I presume you ate after the other officer did?"

"Yes, that's so."

"How long after?"

Dun's eyes narrowed. "About half an hour, I'd say. Maybe a little more, but not much." The point of the doctor's question suddenly hit him. He sat upright with a jerk and slapped the top of the control column with the flat of his hand. "Holy smoke, that's right. I had fish too."

"D'you feel all right?"

The captain nodded. "Yes. Yes, I feel okay."

"Good." Relief showed in Baird's voice. "As soon as I've got my bag I'll give you an emetic."

"Will that get rid of it?"

"Depends. You can't have digested it all yet. Anyway, it doesn't follow that everyone who ate fish will be affected—logic doesn't enter into these things. You could be the one to avoid trouble."

"I'd better be," muttered Dun, staring now into the moonglow ahead.

"Now listen," said Baird. "Is there any way of locking the controls of this airplane?"

"Why yes," said Dun. "There's the automatic pilot. But that wouldn't get us down——"

"I suggest you switch it on, or whatever you do, just in case. If you do happen to feel ill, yell for me immediately. I don't know that I can do much, but if you do get any symptoms they'll come on fast."

The knuckles of Dun's hands gleamed white as he gripped the control column. "Okay," he said quietly. "What about Miss Benson, the stewardess?"

"She's all right. She had meat."

"Well, that's something. Look, for heaven's sake

hurry with that emetic. I can't take any chances, flying this ship."

"Benson is hurrying. Unless I'm mistaken there are at least two people back there in a state of deep shock. One more thing," Baird said, looking straight at the captain. "Are you absolutely certain that we've no other course but to go on?"

"Certain," answered Dun instantly. "I've checked and double-checked. Thick cloud and ground fog until the other side of the mountains. Calgary, Edmonton, Lethbridge—all closed to traffic. That's routine, when ground visibility is zero. In the normal way, it wouldn't worry us."

"Well, it worries us now."

The doctor stepped back to leave, but Dun shot at him, "Just a minute." As the doctor paused, he went on, "I'm in charge of this flight and I must know the facts. Lay it on the line. What are the chances that I'll be all right?"

Baird shook his head angrily, his composure momentarily deserting him. "I wouldn't know," he said savagely. "You just can't apply any rules to a thing like this."

He was halted again before he could leave the flight deck.

"Oh, Doctor."

"Yes?"

"Glad you're aboard."

Baird left without another word. Dun took a deep breath, thinking over what had been said and searching in his mind for a possible course of action. Not for the first time in his flying career, he felt himself in the grip of an acute sense of apprehension, only this time his awareness of his responsibility for the safety of a huge, complex aircraft and nearly sixty lives was tinged with a sudden icy premonition of disaster. Was this, then, what it felt like? Older pilots, those who had been in combat in the war, always maintained that if you kept at the game long enough you'd buy it in the end. How was it that in the space of half an hour a normal, everyday, routine flight, carrying a crowd of happy football fans, could change into a nightmare nearly four miles above the earth, something that would shriek across the front pages of a hundred newspapers?

He pushed the thoughts from him in violent self-disgust. There were things to do, things requiring his complete concentration. Putting out his right hand he flicked the switches on the automatic pilot panel, waiting until each control became fully orientated and the appropriate indicator light gleamed to show that the next stage of the switching over could be started. Ailerons first, needing a slight adjustment of the compensating dial to bring them fully under electrical control; then rudder and elevators were nursed until all the four lights set into the top of the panel had ceased winking and settled down to a steady glow. Satisfied, Dun glanced at his p.d.i. dial and took his hands off the wheel. Sitting back in his seat, he let the aircraft fly itself while he carried out a thorough cockpit check. To an inexperienced eye, the flight deck presented a weird sight. Just as though two invisible men sat in the pilots' seats, the twin control columns moved slightly forward, backwards, then forward again. Compensating the air currents as they gently buffeted the aircraft, the rudder bar moved also, as if of its own volition. Across the great spread of the dual instument panel the dozens of needles each registered its own particular story.

His check completed, he reached for the microphone that hung on its hook beside his head. He quickly clipped it to his neck and adjusted the padded earphones. The boom mike swung round at his touch so that the thin steel curve almost caressed his cheek. Aggressively, he blew at his mustache, puffing it up so that it practically touched his nose. Well, he thought to himself, here goes.

The switch was at send and his voice sounded calm and unhurried.

"Hullo, Vancouver Control. This is Maple Leaf Charter Flight 714. I have an emergency message. I have an emergency message."

His earphones crackled instantly: "Maple Leaf Charter Flight 714. Come in please."

"Vancouver Control. This is Flight 714. Listen. We have three serious cases of suspected food poisoning on board, including the first officer, and possibly others. When we land we shall want ambulances and medical help standing by. Please warn hospitals near the airfield. We're not sure but we think the poisoning may have been caused by the fish served on board at dinner. You'd better put a ban on all food coming from the same source until the trouble has been definitely located. We understand that owing to our late arrival at Winnipeg the food was not supplied by the regular airline contractor. Please check. Is this understood?"

He listened to the acknowledgment, his eyes gazing bleakly at the frozen sea of cloud below and ahead. Vancouver Control sounded as crisp and impersonal as ever but he could guess at the verbal bomb he had exploded down there on the far western seaboard and the burst of activity his words would have triggered off. Almost wearily, he ended the transmission and leaned back in his seat. He felt strangely heavy and tired, as if lead had begun to flow into his limbs. The instrument dials, as his eyes ran automatically over them, seemed to recede until they were far, far away. He was conscious of a cold film of sweat on his forehead and he shivered in a sudden uncontrollable spasm. Then, in a renewal of anger at the perfidy of his body at such a time of crisis, he flung himself with all his strength and concentration into rechecking their flight path, their estimated time of arrival, the expected cross winds over the mountains, the runway plan of Vancouver. He had little idea whether it was a few minutes or several before his preparations were complete. He reached for his log book, opened it and looked at his wrist watch. With a dull and painful slowness his mind began to grapple with the seemingly Herculean task of trying to fix times to the events of the night.

Back in the body of the aircraft, Dr. Baird tucked fresh dry blankets round the limp form of Mrs. Childer and tossed the others out into the aisle. The woman lay back helplessly, her eyes closed, dry lips apart and trembling, moaning quietly. The top of her dress was stained and damp. As Baird watched her she was seized with a fresh paroxysm. Her eyes did not open.

Baird spoke to her husband. "Keep her mopped up and as dry as you can. And warm. She must be warm."

Childer reached up and grabbed the doctor by

the wrist. "For God's sake, Doctor, what's happening?" His voice was shrill. "She's pretty bad, isn't she?"

Baird looked again at the woman. Her breathing was rapid and shallow. "Yes," he said, "she is."

"Well, can't we *do* something for her—give her something."

Baird shook his head. "She needs drugs we haven't got—antibiotics. There's nothing we can do right now but keep her warm."

"But surely even some water——"

"No. She'd gag on it. Your wife is nearly unconscious, Childer. Hold it, now," Baird added hastily as the other man half rose in alarm. "That's nature's own anesthetic. Don't worry. She'll be all right. Your job is to watch her and keep her warm. Even when she's unconscious she'll probably still try to throw up. I'll be back."

Baird moved to the next row of seats. A middle-aged man, collar undone and hands clasping his stomach, sat slumped partly out of his seat, head thrown back and turning from side to side, his face glistening with sweat. He looked up at the doctor, drawing back his lips in a rictus of pain.

"It's murder," the man mumbled. "I never felt like this before."

Baird took a pencil from his jacket pocket and held it in front of the man.

"Listen to me," he said. "I want you to take this pencil."

The man raised his arm with an effort. His fingers tried fumblingly to grasp the pencil but it slipped through them. Baird's eyes narrowed. He lifted the man into a more comfortable position and tucked a blanket in tightly around him.

"I can't hold myself," the man said, "and my head feels like it's in a vise."

"Doctor," someone shouted, "can you come here, please!"

"Wait a minute," Baird called back. "I'll see everyone in turn who wants me."

The stewardess hurried towards him holding a leather bag.

"Good girl," said Baird. "That's the one. Not that I can do much . . ." His voice trailed away as he thought hard. "Where's your p.a. system?" he asked.

"I'll show you," said Janet. She led the way aft to the galley and pointed to a small microphone. "How is Mrs. Childer, Doctor?" she asked.

Baird pursed his lips. "Don't let's pretend otherwise—she's seriously ill," he said. "And if I'm not very much mistaken there are others who'll be as bad before long."

"Do you still think it's food poisoning?" Janet's cheeks were very pale.

"Tolerably certain. Staphylococcal, I'd say, though some of the symptoms out there could indicate even worse. There again, the poisoning could have been caused by salmonella bacilli—who can say, without a proper diagnosis."

"Are you going to give round an emetic?"

"Yes, except of course to those who are already sick. That's all I can do. What we probably need are antibiotics like chloramphenicol, but it's no use thinking about that." Lifting the telephone, Baird paused. "As soon as you can," he told her, "I suggest you organize some help to clean up a bit in there. Squirt plenty of disinfectant around if you've any. Oh, and as you speak to the sick passengers you'd better tell them to forget the conventions and not to lock the door of the toilet—we don't want any passing out in there." He thought for a moment, then pressed the button of the microphone, holding it close. "Ladies and gentlemen, may I have your attention, please? Your attention, please." He heard the murmur of voices die away, leaving only the steady drone of the engines. "First of all, I should introduce myself," he went on. "My name is Baird and I'm a doctor. Some of you are wondering what this malady is that has stricken our fellow passengers and I think it's time everyone knew what is happening and what I'm doing. Well, as far as I can tell with the limited facilities at my disposal we have several cases of food poisoning on board and by deduction—a deduction that has yet to be confirmed—I believe the cause of it to be the fish which was served to some of us at dinner." An excited hubbub broke out at his words. "Now listen to me, please," he said. "There is no cause for alarm. I repeat, there is no cause for alarm. The passengers who have suffered these attacks are being cared for by the stewardess and myself, and the captain has radioed ahead for more medical help to be standing by when we land. If you ate fish for dinner it doesn't necessarily follow that you are going to be affected too. There's seldom any hard and fast rule about this sort of thing and it's perfectly possible that you'll be entirely immune. However, we *are* going to take some precautions and the stewardess and I are coming round to you all. I want you to tell us if you ate fish. Remember, only if you ate fish. If you did, we'll tell you how you can help yourselves. Now, if you'll all settle down we'll begin right away." Baird took his finger off the button and turned to Janet. "All we can really do now is to give immediate first aid," he said.

Janet nodded. "You mean the pills, Doctor?"

"There are two things we can do. We don't know definitely what the source of the poisoning is but we can assume it's been taken internally, so to begin with everyone who had fish must drink several glasses of water—I mean those who are not too ill, of course. That will help to dilute the poison and relieve the toxic effects. After that we'll give an emetic. If there aren't enough pills in my bag to go round we'll have to use salt. Have you plenty of that?"

"I've only got a few small packets that go with the lunches but we can break them open."

"Good. We'll see how far the pills go first. I'll start at the back here with the pills and you begin bringing drinking water to those people already affected, will you? Take some to the first officer too. You'll need help."

Stepping out of the galley, Baird practically cannoned into the lean, lugubrious Englishman called 'Otpot.

"Anything I can do, Doctor?" His voice was concerned.

Baird allowed himself a smile. "Thanks. First, what did you have for dinner?"

"Meat, thank heaven," breathed 'Otpot fervently.

"Right. We're not going to worry about you then for the moment. Will you help the stewardess to hand water round to the passengers who are sick? I want them to drink at least three glasses if they can—more, if possible."

'Otpot entered the galley, returning Janet's

rather tired little smile. In normal circumstances that smile of hers could be guaranteed to quicken the pulse of any airline staff but on this occasion the man beside her could see the hint of fear that lay behind it. He winked at her.

"Don't you worry, miss. Everything's going to be all right."

Janet looked at him gratefully. "I'm sure it is, thanks. Look, here's the water tap and there are the cups, Mr.——"

"The boys call me 'Otpot."

" 'Otpot?" repeated Janet incredulously.

"Yes, Lancashire 'Otpot—you know."

"Oh!" Janet burst out laughing.

"There, that's better. Now, where are t'cups, you say? Come on, lass, let's get started. A fine airline this is. Gives you your dinner, then asks for it back again."

It takes a very great deal to upset the equilibrium of a modern airport. Panic is a thing unknown in such places and would be ruthlessly stamped out if it occurred, for it can be a highly lethal activity.

The control room at Vancouver, when Dun's emergency call began to come through, presented a scene of suppressed excitement. In front of the radio panel an operator wearing headphones transcribed Dun's incoming message straight on to a typewriter, pausing only to reach over and punch an alarm bell on his desk. He carried on imperturbably as a second man appeared behind him, craning over his shoulder to read the words as they were pounded on to the sheet of paper in the typewriter. The newcomer, summoned by the bell, was the airport controller, a tall, lean man who

had spent a lifetime in the air and knew the conditions of travel over the northern hemisphere as
well as he knew his own back garden. Better, in
fact, for didn't his onions always run to seed? He
got halfway through the message, then stepped
sharply back, cracking an order over his shoulder
to the telephone operator on the far side of the
room.

"Get me Air Traffic Control quickly. Then clear
the teletype circuit to Winnipeg. Priority message."
The controller picked up a phone, waited a few
seconds, then said, "Vancouver controller here."
His voice was deceptively unhurried. "Maple Leaf
Charter Flight 714 from Winnipeg to Vancouver
reports emergency. Serious food poisoning among
the passengers, and I mean serious. The first officer
is down with it too. Better clear all levels below
them for priority approach and landing. Can do?
Good. ETA is 05.05." The controller glanced at
the wall clock; it read 02.15. "Right. We'll keep
you posted." He pushed down the telephone cradle
with his thumb, keeping it there as he barked at
the teletype operator, "Got Winnipeg yet? Good.
Send this message. Starts: 'Controller Winnipeg.
Urgent. Maple Leaf Charter Flight 714 reports
serious food poisoning among passengers and crew
believed due to fish served dinner on flight. Imperative check source and suspend all other food service originating same place. Understand source was
not, repeat not, regular airline caterer.' That's
all." He swung round to the telephone switchboard again. "Get me the local manager of Maple
Leaf Charter. Burdick's his name. After that I
want the city police—senior officer on duty." He
leaned over the radio operator's shoulder again

and finished reading the now completed message. "Acknowledge that, Greg. Tell them that all altitudes below them are being cleared and that they'll be advised of landing instructions later. We shall want further news later of the condition of those passengers, too."

On the floor below, an operator of the Government of Canada Western Air Traffic Control swiveled in his chair to call across the room, "What's in Green One between here and Calgary?"

"Westbound. There's an air force North Star at 18,000. Just reported over Penticton. Maple Leaf 714——"

"714's in trouble. They want all altitudes below them cleared."

"The North Star's well ahead and there's nothing close behind. There's an eastbound Constellation ready for take-off."

"Clear it, but hold any other eastbound traffic for the time being. Bring the North Star straight in when it arrives."

Upstairs, the controller had scooped up the telephone again, holding it with one hand as the other pulled at his necktie, worrying the knot free. Irritably he threw the length of red silk on the table. "Hullo, Burdick? Controller here. Look, we've got an emergency on one of your flights—714 ex Toronto and Winnipeg. Eh? No, the aircraft's all right. The first officer and several passengers are down with food poisoning. I called Winnipeg right away. Told them to trace the source of the food. Apparently it isn't the usual caterer. No, that's right. See here, you'd better come over as soon as you can." He jabbed the telephone cradle again with his thumb and nodded to the switchboard operator. "The police—got them yet? Good, put them on. Hullo, this is the controller, Vancouver Airport. Who am I speaking to, please? Look, Inspector, we have an emergency on an incoming flight. Several of the passengers and one of the crew have been taken ill with food poisoning and we need ambulances and doctors out here at the airport. Eh? Three serious, possibly others—be prepared for plenty. The flight is due in just after five o'clock local time—in about two and a half hours. Will you alert the hospitals, get the ambulances, set up a traffic control? Right. We'll be on again as soon as we've got more information."

Within five minutes Harry Burdick had arrived, puffing into the room. The local Maple Leaf manager was a portly little man with an abundant supply of body oils; inexhaustible, it seemed, for no one had ever seen him without his face streaked with runnels of perspiration. He stood in the center of the room, his jacket over his arm, gasping for breath after his hurry and swabbing the lunar-scope of his face with a great blue-spotted handkerchief.

"Where's the message?" he grunted. He ran his eye quickly over the sheet of paper the radio operator handed to him. "How's the weather at Calgary?" he asked the controller. "It would be quicker to go in there, wouldn't it?"

"No good, I'm afraid. There's fog right down to the grass everywhere east of the Rockies as far as Manitoba. They'll have to come through."

A clerk called across from his phone, "Passenger agent wants to know when we'll be resuming east-bound traffic. Says should he keep the passengers downtown or bring 'em out here?"

Burdick shook a worried head. "Where's the last position report?" he demanded. A clipboard was passed to him and he scanned it anxiously.

The controller called back to the clerk, "Tell him to keep them downtown. We don't want a mob out here. We'll give him lots of warning when we're ready."

"You say you've got medical help coming?" asked Burdick.

"Yes," replied the controller. "The city police are working on that. They'll alert the hospitals and see to the arrangements when we get the plane here."

Burdick clicked a fat finger. "Hey! That message now. They say the first officer is down, so presumably the captain passed the message. Is he affected at all? Better ask, Controller. And while you're about it, I should check whether there's a doctor on board. You never know. Tell them we're getting medical advice here in case they need it."

The controller nodded and picked up the stand microphone from the radio desk. Before he could begin, Burdick called, "Say, suppose the captain does take sick, Controller? Who's going to . . ."

He left the sentence unfinished as the level gaze of the man opposite met his.

"I'm not supposing anything," said the controller. "I'm praying, that's all. Let's hope those poor devils up there are praying too."

Exhaling noisily, Burdick dug in his pockets for cigarettes. "Joe," he said to the switchboard operator, "get me Dr. Davidson, will you? You'll find his number on the emergency list."

FOUR

0220—0245

NEARLY FOUR MILES above the earth, the aircraft held her course.

In every direction, as far as the eye could see, stretched the undulating carpet of cloud, passing beneath the great machine so slowly as to make it appear almost stationary. It was a cold, empty, utterly lonely world, a world in which the heart-beating throb of the aircraft's engines came rumbling back from the silver-tinted wastes.

Far below, that same powerful pulse of engines, in normal weather, would have reverberated through the desolate valleys of the Rocky Mountains. Tonight, muffled by the ground fog, the sound of her passing was not enough to disturb the scattered communities as they slept in their remote farmsteads. Had someone there chanced to hear the aircraft, he may have disregarded it as an event too commonplace to be worthy of thought. Or he may have wished himself up there, flying to some faraway place and enjoying the solicitous attentions of a crew whose primary concern was his safety and comfort. He could not have dreamed that practically everyone in the aircraft would have gladly and gratefully changed places with him.

49

Like a monstrous weed, fear was taking root in the minds of most of the passengers. There were some who probably still failed to realize exactly what was going on. But most of them, especially those who could hear the groans and retching of the ones who were ill, felt the presence of a terrible crisis. The doctor's words over the public address system, once they had sunk in, had provided plenty to think about. The hubbub of dismay and conjecture following them had soon died away, to be replaced by whispers and uneasy snatches of conversation.

Baird had given Janet two pills. "Take them to the captain," he told her in a low voice. "Tell him to drink as much water as he can. If the poison is in his system the water will help dilute it. Then he's to take the pills. They'll make him sick—that's what they're for."

When Janet entered the flight deck Dun was completing a radio transmission. He signed off and gave her a strained grin. Neither of them was deluded by it.

"Hullo, Jan," he said. His hand was shaking slightly. "This is becoming quite a trip. Vancouver has just been asking for more details. I thought this lot would shake them up a bit. How are things back there?"

"So far, so good," said Janet as lightly as she could. She held out the pills. "Doctor says you're to drink as much as you can, then take these. They'll make you feel a bit green."

"What a prospect." He reached down into the deep seat pocket at his side and took out a water bottle. "Well, down the hatch." After a long draught, he swallowed the pills, pulling a wry face.

"Never could take those things—and they tasted awful."

Janet looked anxiously down at him as he sat before the flickering panel of gauges and dials, the two control columns moving spasmodically backwards and forwards in the eerie grip of the automatic pilot. She touched his shoulder.

"How do you feel?" she asked. His pallor, the beads of perspiration on his forehead, did not escape her. She prayed to herself that it was just the strain he was undergoing.

"Me?" His tone was unnaturally hearty. "I'm fine. What about you? Had your pills yet?"

"I don't need any. I had chops for dinner."

"You were wise. From now on I think I'll be a vegetarian—it's safer that way." He turned in his seat and looked over at the first officer, now prone on the floor, his head on a pillow. "Poor old Pete," he murmured. "I sure hope he's going to be all right."

"That's up to you, isn't it, Captain?" said Janet urgently. "The faster you can push this thing into Vancouver, the quicker we'll get him and the others into hospital." She stepped over to Pete and bent down to adjust a blanket round him, hiding the sudden tremble of tears that threatened to break through her reserve. Dun was troubled as he regarded her.

"You think a lot of him, Jan, don't you?" he said.

Her golden head moved a little.

"I—I suppose so," she replied. "I've got to like him during the past few months since he joined the crew and this—this horrible business has made me . . ." She checked herself and jumped up. "I've

51

a lot to do. Have to hold a few noses while the doctor pours water down their gullets. Not very popular, I imagine, with some of those hard-drinking types."

She smiled quickly at him and opened the door to the passenger deck. Baird was halfway along the starboard side, talking to a middle-aged couple who stared at him nervously.

"Doctor," the woman was saying intently, "that young girl, the stewardess—I've seen her keep going up to the pilots' cabin. Are they well? I mean, supposing they're taken ill too—what will happen to us?" She clutched at her husband. "Hector, I'm frightened. I wish we hadn't come——"

"Now, now, dear, take it easy," said her husband with an assurance he obviously didn't feel. "There's no danger, I'm sure, and nothing has happened so far." He turned baggy, horn-rimmed eyes on the doctor. "*Did* the pilots have fish?"

"Not all the fish was necessarily infected," answered Baird evasively. "Anyway, we don't know for certain that the fish was to blame. You've nothing to worry about—we'll take great care of the crew. Now, sir, did you have fish or meat?"

The man's bulbous eyes seemed about to depart from their sockets. "Fish," he exclaimed. "We both ate fish." Indignation welled up in him. "I think it's disgraceful that such a thing can happen. There ought to be an inquiry."

"I can assure you there will be, whatever the cause." Baird handed them each a pill, which they accepted as gingerly as if it were high explosive. "Now, you'll be brought a jug of water. Drink three glasses each—four, if you can manage them. Then take the pill. It'll make you sick, but that's what it's for. Don't worry about it. There are paper bags in the seat pockets."

He left the couple staring hypnotically at their pills and in a few minutes, progressing along the rows, had reached his own empty seat with Spencer sitting alongside it.

"Meat," said Spencer promptly, before Baird could put the question.

"Good for you," said the doctor. "That's one less to worry about."

"You're having a heavy time of it, Doc, aren't you?" Spencer commented. "Can you do with any help?"

"I can do with all the help in the world," growled Baird. "But there's not much you can do, unless you'd like to give Miss Benson and the other fellow a hand with the water."

"Sure I will." Spencer lowered his voice. "Someone back there sounds in a bad way."

"They *are* in a bad way. The devil of it is," said Baird bitterly, "I've got nothing I can give them that's of any real use. You make a trip to a ball game—you don't think to pack your bag in case a dozen people get taken sick with food poisoning on the way. I've a hypodermic and morphia—never travel without *those*—but here they may do more harm than good. God knows why I threw in a bottle of emetic pills, but it's a good thing I did. Some dramamine would be mighty useful now."

"What does that do?"

"In these cases the serious thing is the loss of body fluids. An injection of dramamine would help to preserve them."

"You mean all this sickness gradually dehydrates a person?"

53

"Exactly."

Spencer rubbed his chin as he digested this information. "Well," he said, "thank God for lamb chops. I just don't feel ready for dehydration yet."

Baird frowned at him. "Perhaps you see some humor in this situation," he said sourly. "I don't. All I can see is complete helplessness while people suffer and steadily get worse."

"Don't ride me, Doc," Spencer protested. "I meant nothing. I'm only too glad we didn't get sick on the fish like the other poor devils."

"Yes, yes, maybe you're right." Baird passed a hand over his eyes. "I'm getting too old for this sort of thing," he muttered, half to himself.

"What do you mean?"

"Never mind, never mind."

Spencer got to his feet. "Now, hold on there, Doc," he said. "You're doing a fine job. The luckiest thing that ever happened to these people is having you on board."

"All right, junior," Baird retorted sarcastically, "you can spare me the salesman's pep talk. I'm not proposing to run out on you."

The younger man flushed slightly. "Fair enough— I asked for that. Well, tell me what I can do. I've been sitting warming my seat while you've been hard at it. You're tired."

"Tired nothing." Baird put his hand on the other man's arm. "Take no notice of me. I worked off a bit of steam on you. Feel better for it. It's knowing what ought to be done and not being able to do it. Makes me a little raw."

"That's okay," Spencer said with a grin. "Glad to be of some use, anyway."

"I'll tell Miss Benson you're willing to help if

54

she needs you. Once the water is all given out, I think maybe you'd better stay where you are. There's more than enough traffic in the aisle already."

"As you say. Well, I'm here if you want me." Spencer resumed his seat. "But tell me—just how serious is all this?"

Baird looked him in the eye. "As serious as you are ever likely to want it," he said curtly.

He moved along to the group of football fans who had earlier in the evening imbibed whisky with such liberality. The quartet was now reduced in strength to three, and one of these sat shivering in his shirt sleeves, a blanket drawn across his chest. His color was gray.

"Keep this man warm," said Baird. "Has he had anything to drink?"

"That's a laugh," replied a man behind him, shuffling a pack of cards. "He must have downed a couple of pints of rye, if I'm any judge."

"Before or after dinner?"

"Both, I reckon."

"That's right," agreed another in the group. "And I thought Harry could hold his liquor."

"In this case it's done him no harm," Baird said. "In fact, it has helped to dilute the poison, I don't doubt. Have any of you men got any brandy?"

"Cleared mine up," said the man with the cards.

"Wait a minute," said the other, leaning forward to get at his hip pocket. "I might have some left in the flask. We gave it a good knocking, waiting about at Toronto."

"Give him a few sips," instructed Baird. "Take it gently. Your friend is very ill."

"Say, Doctor," said the man with the cards, "what's the score? Are we on schedule?"

"As far as I know, yes."

"This puts paid to the ball game for Andy, eh?"

"It certainly does. We'll get him to hospital just as soon as we land."

"Poor old Andy," commiserated the man with the hip flask, unscrewing the cap, "he always was an unlucky so-and-so. Hey," he exclaimed as a thought struck him, "you say he's pretty bad—he'll be all right, won't he?"

"I hope so. You'd better pay him some attention, as I said, and make sure he doesn't throw off those blankets."

"Fancy this happening to old Andy. What about 'Otpot, that English screwball? You drafted him?"

"Yes, he's giving us a hand." As Baird stepped away the man with the cards flicked them irritably in his hand and demanded of his companion, "How d'you like this for a two-day vacation?"

Further along the aisle, Baird found Janet anxiously bending over Mrs. Childer. He raised one of the woman's eyelids. She was unconscious.

Her husband seized frantically on the doctor's presence.

"How is she?" he implored.

"She's better off now than when she was conscious and in pain," said Baird, hoping he sounded convincing. "When the body can't take any more, nature pulls down the shutter."

"Doctor, I'm scared. I've never seen her so ill. Just what is this fish poisoning? What caused it? I know it was the fish, but why?"

Baird hesitated.

"Well," he said slowly, "I guess you've a right to

56

know. It's a very serious illness, one that needs treatment at the earliest possible moment. We're doing all we can right now."

"I know you are, Doctor, and I'm grateful. She is going to be okay, isn't she? I mean——"

"Of course she is," said Baird gently. "Try not to worry. There'll be an ambulance waiting to take her to hospital immediately we land. Then it's only a question of treatment and time before she's perfectly well again."

"My God," said Childer, heaving a deep breath, "it's good to hear you say that." Yes, thought Baird, but supposing I had the common guts to put it the other way? "But listen," Childer suggested, "couldn't we divert—you know, put down at a nearer airport?"

"We thought of that," answered Baird, "but there's a ground fog which would make landing at other fields highly dangerous. Anyway, we've now passed them and we're over the Rockies. No, the quickest way of getting your wife under proper care is to crack on for Vancouver as fast as we can, and that's what we're doing."

"I see ... You still think it was the fish, do you, Doctor?"

"At present I've no means of telling for certain, but I think so. Food poisoning can be caused either by the food just spoiling—the medical name is staphylococcal poisoning—or it's possible that some toxic substance has accidentally gotten into it during its preparation."

"What kind do you think this is, Doctor?" asked a passenger in the next row who had been straining to hear Baird's words.

"I can't be sure, but from the effect that it's had

57

on the folk here I'd suspect the second cause rather than the first—a toxic substance, that is."

"And you don't know what it is?"

"I have no idea. We won't know until we're able to make proper tests in a laboratory. With modern methods of handling food—and especially the careful way in which airlines prepare food—the chances of this happening are a million to one against. We just happen to be unfortunate. I can tell you, though, that our dinner tonight didn't come from the usual caterers. Something went wrong owing to our late arrival at Winnipeg and another firm supplied us. That may or may not have a bearing on it."

Childer nodded, turning the conversation over in his mind. Funny how people seem to find comfort in a medical man's words, Baird reflected in a sardonic appraisal of himself. Even when what a doctor has to say is bad news, the fact that he has said it seems to be reassuring to them. He's the doctor; he won't let it happen. Maybe we haven't come so far from witchcraft, he thought to himself with a touch of anger; there's always the doctor with his box of magic, to pull something out of the hat. Most of his life had been spent in nursing, coaxing, bullying, cajoling—reassuring frightened and trusting people that he knew best, and hoping each time that his old skill and sometimes very necessary bluff had not deserted him. Well, this could be the moment of truth, the final, inescapable challenge which he had always known would face him one day.

He felt Janet standing beside him. He questioned her with his eyes, sensing her to be on the edge of hysteria.

"Two more passengers have been taken ill, Doctor. At the back there."

"Are you sure it isn't just the pills?"

"Yes, I'm quite sure."

"Right. I'll get to them straight away. Will you have another look at the first officer, Miss Benson? He might feel like a little water."

He had barely reached the two new cases and begun his examination before Janet was back again.

"Doctor, I'm terribly worried. I think you ought to——"

The buzz of the galley intercom cut across her words like a knife. She stood transfixed as the buzz continued without a break. Baird was the first to move.

"Don't bother with that thing," he rapped out. "Quick!"

Moving with an agility quite foreign to him, he raced along the aisle and burst into the flight deck. There he paused momentarily, while his eyes and brain registered what had happened, and in that instant something inside him, something mocking in its tone but menacing too, said: *You were right—this is it.*

The captain was rigid in his seat, sweat masking his face and streaking the collar of his uniform. One hand clutched at his stomach. The other was pressed on the intercom button on the wall beside him.

In two bounds the doctor reached him and leaned over the back of the seat, supporting him under the armpits. Dun was swearing between his clenched teeth, quietly and viciously.

"Take it easy, now," said Baird. "We'd better get you away from there."

"I did ... what you said ..." Dun gasped, closing his eyes and squeezing the words out in painful jerks. "It was too late. ... Give me something, Doc. ... Give me something, quickly. ... Got to hold out ... get us down ... She's on autopilot but ... got to get down. ... Must tell Control .. must tell ..." His mouth moved silently. With a desperate effort he tried to speak. Then his eyes rolled up and he collapsed.

"Quick, Miss Benson," called Baird. "Help me get him out."

Panting and struggling, they pulled Dun's heavy body out of the pilot's seat and eased him on to the floor alongside the first officer. Swiftly, Baird took out his stethoscope and made an examination. In a matter of seconds Janet had produced coats and a blanket; as soon as the doctor had finished she made a pillow for the captain and wrapped him round. She was trembling as she stood up again.

"Can you do what he asked, Doctor? Can you bring him round long enough to land the plane?"

Baird thrust his instruments back into his pockets. He looked at the banks of dials and switches, at the control columns still moving of their own accord. In the dim light from the battery of dials his features seemed suddenly much older, and unbearably weary.

"You are part of this crew, Miss Benson, so I'll be blunt." His voice was so hard that she flinched. "Can you face some unpleasant facts?"

"I—I think so." In spite of herself, she faltered.

"Very well. Unless I can get all these people to a

hospital quickly—very quickly—I can't even be sure of saving their lives."

"But . . ."

"They need stimulants, intravenous injections for shock. The captain too. He's held out too long."

"Is he very bad?"

"It will soon become critical—and that goes for the others as well."

Barley audible, Janet whispered, "Doctor—what are we going to do?"

"Let me ask you a question. How many passengers are on board?"

"Fifty-six."

"How many fish dinners did you serve?"

Janet struggled to remember. "About fifteen, I think. More people had meat than fish, and some didn't eat at all as it was so late."

"I see."

Baird regarded her steadily. When he spoke again his voice was harsh, almost belligerent.

"Miss Benson, did you ever hear of long odds?"

Janet tried to focus on what he was saying.

"Long odds? Yes, I suppose so. I don't know what it means."

"I'll tell you," said Baird. "It means this. Out of a total field of fifty-six our one chance of survival depends on there being a person aboard this airplane who is not only qualified to land it but who also didn't have fish for dinner tonight."

His words hung between them as they stood there, staring at each other.

FIVE

0245—0300

CALMNESS, like an anodyne cushioning the shock, descended on Janet as the words of the doctor penetrated her mind. She met his eyes steadily, well aware of his unspoken injunction to prepare herself for death.

Until now part of her had refused to accept what was happening. While she busied herself tending the passengers and trying to comfort the sick, something had insisted that this was an evil nightmare, the sort of dream in which an everyday sequence of events is suddenly deflected into one of mounting horror by some totally unexpected but quite logical incident. At any moment, her inner voice had told her, she would wake up to find half the bedclothes on the floor and the traveling clock on her locker buzzing to herald another early-morning scramble to get ready before take-off.

Now that sense of unreality was swept away. She knew it was happening, really happening, to her, Janet Benson, the pretty twenty-one-year-old blonde who had learned to expect the turning glances of airport staff as she walked briskly along the pine-smelling corridors. Fear had gone from her, at least for the moment. She wondered, in the passing thought of an instant, what her family at home were doing, how it was possible for her life to be extinguished in a few seconds' madness of shrieking metal without those who had borne her feeling even a tremor as they slept peacefully a thousand miles away.

"I understand, Doctor," she said levelly.

"Do you know of anyone on board with any experience of flying?"

She cast her mind over the passenger list, recalling the names. "There's no one from the airline," she said. "I don't know ... about anyone else. I suppose I'd better start asking."

"Yes, you'd better," said Baird slowly. "Whatever you do, try not to alarm them. Otherwise we may start a panic. Some of them know the first officer is sick. Just say the captain wondered if there's someone with flying experience who could help with the radio."

"Very well, Doctor," said Janet quietly. "I'll do that."

She hesitated, as Baird obviously had something more to say. "Miss Benson—what's your first name?" he asked.

"Janet."

He nodded. "Janet—I think I made some remark earlier on about your training. It was unjustified and unforgivable—the comment of a stupid old man who could have done with more training himself. I'd like to take it back."

Some of the color returned to her cheeks as she smiled. "I'd forgotten it," she said. She moved towards the door, anxious to begin her questioning and to know the worst as quickly as she could. But Baird's face was puckered in an effort of concentration, as if something at the back of his mind was eluding him. He frowned at the painted emergency-escape instructions on the side of the cabin, not seeing them.

"Wait," he told her.

"Yes?" She paused, her hand on the catch of the door.

He snapped his fingers and turned to her. "I've got it. I knew someone had spoken to me about airplanes. That young fellow in the seat next to mine—the one who joined us at the last minute at Winnipeg——"

"Mr. Spencer?"

"That's him. George Spencer. I forget exactly but he seemed to know something about flying. Get him up here, will you? Don't tell him more than I've just said—we don't want the other passengers to know the truth. But carry on asking them too, in case there's someone else."

"He just offered to help me," said Janet, "so he must be unaffected by the food."

"Yes, you're right," exclaimed Baird. "We both had meat. Get him, Janet."

He paced the narrow cabin nervously while she was gone, then knelt to feel the pulse of the captain lying prone and unconscious beside the first officer. At the first sound of the door behind him he jumped to his feet, blocking the entrance. Spencer stood there, looking at him in bewilderment.

"Hullo, Doc," the young man greeted him. "What's this about the radio?"

"Are you a pilot?" Baird shot out, not moving.

"A long time ago. In the war. I wouldn't know about radio procedures now, but if the captain thinks I can——"

"Come in," said Baird.

He stepped aside, closing the door quickly behind the young man. Spencer's head snapped up at the sight of the pilots' empty seats and the controls moving by themselves. Then he wheeled round to the two men stretched on the floor under their blankets.

"No!" he gasped. "Not both of them?"

"Yes," said Baird shortly, "both of them."

Spencer seemed hardly able to believe his eyes. "But—man alive"—he stuttered—"when did it happen?"

"The captain went down a few minutes ago. They both had fish."

Spencer put out a hand to steady himself, leaning against a junction box of cables on the wall.

"Listen," said Baird urgently. "Can you fly this aircraft—and land it?"

"No!" Shock stabbed at Spencer's voice. "Definitely no! Not a chance!"

"But you just said you flew in the war," Baird insisted.

"That was thirteen years ago. I haven't touched a plane since. And I was on fighters—tiny Spitfires about an eighth of the size of this ship and with only one engine. This has four. The flying characteristics are completely different."

Spencer's fingers, shaking slightly, probed his jacket for cigarettes, found a packet, and shook one out. Baird watched him as he lit up.

"You could have a go at it," he pressed.

Spencer shook his head angrily. "I tell you, the idea's crazy," he snapped. "You don't know what's involved. I wouldn't be able to take in a Spitfire

65

now, let alone this." He jabbed his cigarette towards the banks of instruments.

"It seems to me flying isn't a thing you'd forget," said Baird, watching him closely.

"It's a different kind of flying altogether. It's—it's like driving an articulated sixteen-wheeler truck in heavy traffic when all you've driven before is a fast sports job on open roads."

"But it's still driving," persisted Baird. Spencer did not answer, taking a long draw on his cigarette. Baird shrugged and half turned away. "Well," he said, "let's hope then there's someone else who can fly this thing—neither of these men can." He looked down at the pilots.

The door opened and Janet came into the flight deck. She glanced inquiringly at Spencer, then back at the doctor. Her voice was flat.

"There's no one else," she said.

"That's it, then," said the doctor. He waited for Spencer to speak, but the younger man was staring forward at the row upon row of luminous dials and switches. "Mr. Spencer," said Baird, measuring his words with deliberation, "I know nothing of flying. All I know is this. There are several people on this plane who will die within a few hours if they don't get to hospital soon. Among those left who are physically able to fly the plane, you are the only one with any kind of qualification to do so." He paused. "What do you suggest?"

Spencer looked from the girl to the doctor. He asked tensely, "You're quite sure there's no chance of either of the pilots recovering in time?"

"None at all, I'm afraid. Unless I can get them to hospital quickly I can't even be sure of saving their lives."

The young salesman exhaled a lungful of smoke and ground the rest of his cigarette under his heel.

"It looks as if I don't have much choice, doesn't it?" he said.

"That's right. Unless you'd rather we carried on until we were out of gas—probably halfway across the Pacific."

"Don't kid yourself this is a better way." Spencer stepped forward to the controls and looked ahead at the white sea of cloud below them, glistening in the moonlight. "Well," he said, "I guess I'm drafted. You've got yourself a new driver, Doc." He slipped into the lefthand pilot's seat and glanced over his shoulder at the two behind him. "If you know any good prayers you'd better start brushing up on them."

Baird moved up to him and slapped his arm lightly. "Good man," he said with feeling.

"What are you going to tell the people back there?" asked Spencer, running his eye over the scores of gauges in front of him and racking his memory to recall some of the lessons he had learned in a past that now seemed very far away.

"For the moment—nothing," answered the doctor.

"Very wise," said Spencer dryly. He studied the bewildering array of instrument dials. "Let's have a look at this mess. The flying instruments must be in front of each pilot. That means that the center panel will probably be engines only. Ah—here we are: altitude 20,000. Level flight. Course 290. We're on automatic pilot—we can be thankful for that. Air speed 210 knots. Throttles, pitch, trim, mixture, landing-gear controls. Flaps? There should be an indicator somewhere. Yes, here it is. Well,

67

they're the essentials anyway—I hope. We'll need a check list for landing, but we can get that on the radio."

"Can you do it?"

"I wouldn't know, Doc—I just wouldn't know. I've never seen a setup like this before in my life. Where are we now, and where are we going?"

"From what the captain said, we're over the Rockies," replied Baird. "He couldn't turn off course earlier because of fog, so we're going through to Vancouver."

"We'll have to find out." Spencer looked about him in the soft glow. "Where *is* the radio control, anyway?"

Janet pointed to a switchbox above his head. "I know they use that to talk to the ground," she told him, "but I don't know which switches you have to set."

"Ah yes, let's see." He peered at the box. "Those are the frequency selectors—we'd better leave them where they are. What's this?—transmit." He clicked over a switch, lighting up a small red bulb. "That's it. First blood to George. Now we're ready for business."

Janet handed him a headset with the boom microphone attached. "I know you press the button on the mike when you speak," she said.

Adjusting the earphones, Spencer spoke to the doctor. "You know, whatever happens I'm going to need a second pair of hands up here in front. You've got your patients to look after, so I think the best choice is Miss Canada here. What do you say?"

Baird nodded. "I agree. Is that all right, Janet?"

68

"I suppose so—but I know nothing of all this." Janet waved helplessly at the control panels.

"Good," said Spencer breezily, "that makes two of us. Sit down and make yourself comfortable—better strap yourself in. You must have watched the pilots quite a lot. They've added a lot of gimmicks since my flying days."

Janet struggled into the first officer's seat, taking care not to touch the control column as it swayed back and forth. There was an anxious knocking on the communication door.

"That's for me," said Baird. "I must get back. Good luck."

He left quickly. Alone with the stewardess, Spencer summoned up a grin.

"Okay?" he asked.

She nodded dumbly, preparing to put on a headset.

"The name's Janet, is it? Mine's George." Spencer's tone became serious. "I won't fool you, Janet. This will be tough."

"I know it."

"Well, let's see if I can send out a distress call. What's our flight number?"

"714."

"Right. Here goes, then." He pressed the button on his microphone. "Mayday, mayday, mayday," he began in an even voice. It was one signal he could never forget. He had called it one murky October afternoon above the French coast, with the tail of his Spitfire all but shot off, and two Hurricanes had mercifully appeared to usher him across the channel like a pair of solicitous old aunts.

"Mayday, mayday, mayday," he continued. "This

is Flight 714, Maple Leaf Air Charter, in distress. Come in, anyone. Over."

He caught his breath as a voice responded immediately over the air.

"Hullo, 714. This is Vancouver. We have been waiting to hear from you. Vancouver to all aircraft: this frequency now closed to all other traffic. Go ahead, 714."

"Thank you, Vancouver. 714. We are in distress. Both pilots and several passengers ... how many passengers, Janet?"

"It was five a few minutes ago. May be more now, though."

"Correction. At least five passengers are suffering from food poisoning. Both pilots are unconscious and in serious condition. We have a doctor with us who says that neither pilot can be revived to fly the aircraft. If they and the passengers are not gotten to hospital quickly it may be fatal for them. Did you get that, Vancouver?"

The voice crackled back instantly, "Go ahead, 714. I'm reading you."

Spencer took a deep breath. "Now we come to the interesting bit. My name is Spencer, George Spencer. I am a passenger on this airplane. Correction: I *was* a passenger. I am now the pilot. For your information I have about a thousand hours total flying time, all of it on single-engined fighters. Also I haven't flown an airplane for nearly thirteen years. So you'd better get someone on this radio who can give me some instructions about flying this thing. Our altitude is 20,000, course 290 magnetic, air speed 210 knots. That's the story. It's your move, Vancouver. Over."

"Vancouver to 714. Stand by."

Spencer wiped the gathering sweat from his forehead and grinned across to Janet. "Want to bet that's caused a bit of stir in the dovecotes down there?" She shook her head, listening intently to her earphones. In a few seconds the air was alive again, the voice as measured and impersonal as before.

"Vancouver to Flight 714. Please check with doctor on board for any possibility of either pilot recovering. This is important. Repeat, this is important. Ask him to do everything possible to revive one of them even if he has to leave the sick passengers. Over."

Spencer pressed his transmit button. "Vancouver, this is Flight 714. Your message is understood, but no go, I'm afraid. The doctor says there is no possibility whatever of pilots recovering to make the landing. He says they are critically ill and may die unless they get hospital treatment soon. Over."

There was a slight pause. Then: "Vancouver Control to 714. Your message understood. Will you stand by, please."

"Roger, Vancouver," acknowledged Spencer and switched off again. He said to Janet, "We can only wait now while they think up what to do."

His hands played nervously with the control column in front of him, following its movements, trying to gauge its responsiveness as he attempted to call up the old cunning in him, the flying skill that had once earned for him quite a reputation in the squadron: three times home on a wing and a prayer. He smiled to himself as he recalled the war-time phrase. But in the next moment, as he looked blankly at the monstrous assembly of wavering needles and the unfamiliar banks of levers and

71

switches, he felt himself in the grip of an icy despair. What had his flying in common with this? This was like sitting in a submarine, surrounded by the meaningless dials and instruments of science fiction. One wrong or clumsy move might shatter in a second the even tenor of their flight; if it did, who was to say that he could bring the aircraft under control again? All the chances were that he couldn't. This time there would be no comforting presence of Hurricanes to shepherd him home. He began to curse the head office which had whipped him away from Winnipeg to go trouble-shooting across to Vancouver at a moment's notice. The prospect of a sales manager's appointment and the lure of a house on Parkway Heights now seemed absurdly trivial and unimportant. It would be damnable to end like this, not to see Mary again, not to say to her all the things that were still unspoken. As for Bobsie and Kit, the life insurance would not take them very far. He should have done more for those poor kids, the world's best.

A movement beside him arrested his thoughts. Janet was kneeling on her seat, looking back to where the still figures of the captain and the first officer lay on the floor.

"One of those a boy friend of yours?" he asked.

"No," said Janet hesitantly, "not really."

"Skip it," said Spencer, a jagged edge to his voice. "I understand. I'm sorry, Janet." He put a cigarette in his mouth and fumbled for matches. "I don't suppose this is allowed, is it, but maybe the airline can stretch a point."

In the sudden flare of the match she could see, very clearly, the fierce burning anger in his eyes.

72

SIX

0300—0325

WITH AN ACCELERATING thunder of engines the last
eastbound aircraft to take off from Vancouver that
night had gathered speed along the wetly gleaming
runway and climbed into the darkness. Its naviga-
tion lights, as it made the required circuit of the
airport, had been shrouded in a damp clinging
mist. Several other aircraft, in process of being
towed back from their dispersal points to bays
alongside the departure buildings, were beaded
with moisture. It was a cold night. Ground staff,
moving about their tasks in the yellow arc lights,
slapped their gloved hands around themselves to
keep warm. None of them spoke more than was
necessary. One slowly taxiing aircraft came to a
stop and cut its engines at a wave from the indicator torches of a ground man facing it in front. In
the sudden silence the swish of its propellers
seemed an intrusion. Normally busy Vancouver
prepared itself with quiet competence for emergency.

Within the brightly lit control room the atmos-
phere was tense with concentration. Replacing his
telephone, the controller lit a cigarette, wreathing
himself in clouds of blue smoke as he studied a
wall map. He turned to Burdick. Perched on the

edge of a table, the plump manager of Maple Leaf Airline had just finished consulting again the clipboard of information he held in his hand.

"Right, Harry," said the controller. His tone was that of a man running over his actions more to satisfy himself that everything had been done rather than to impart information to another. "As of now, I'm holding all departures for the east. We've got nearly an hour in which to clear the present outgoing traffic in other directions, leaving plenty of time in hand. After that everything scheduled outwards must wait until . . . until afterwards, anyway." The telephone buzzed. He snatched it up. "Yes? I see. Warn all stations and aircraft that we can accept incoming flights for the next forty-five minutes only. Divert everything with an ETA later than that. All traffic must be kept well away from the east-west lane between Calgary and here. Got that? Good." He dropped the instrument back into its cradle and addressed an assistant who sat also holding a telephone. "Have you raised the fire chief yet?"

"Ringing his home now."

"Tell him he'd better get here—it looks like a big show. And ask the duty fire officer to notify the city fire department. They may want to move equipment into the area."

"I've done that. Vancouver Control here," said the assistant into his telephone. "Hold the line, please." He cupped his hand over the mouthpiece. "Shall I alert the Air Force?"

"Yes. Have them keep the zone clear of their aircraft."

Burdick hitched himself off the table. "That's a

thought," he said. Great damp patches stretched from the armpits of his shirt.

"Have you any pilots here at the airport?" asked the controller.

Burdick shook his head. "Not one," he said. "We'll have to get help."

The controller thought rapidly. "Try Cross-Canada. They have most of their men based here. Explain the position. We'll need a man fully experienced with this type of aircraft who is capable of giving instruction over the air."

"Do you think there's a chance?"

"I don't know, but we've got to try. Can you suggest anything else?"

"No," said Burdick, "I can't. But I sure don't envy him that job."

The switchboard operator called, "The city police again. Will you take them?"

"Put them on," said the controller.

"I'll see the Cross-Canada people," said Burdick. "And I must ring Montreal and tell my chief what's happening."

"Do it through the main board, will you?" asked the controller. "The one in here is getting snarled up." He lifted the telephone as Burdick hurried out of the room. "Controller speaking. Ah, Inspector, I'm glad it's you. Yes ... yes ... that's fine. Now listen, Inspector. We're in bad trouble, much worse than we thought. First, we may have to ask you if one of your cars can collect a pilot in town and bring him here just as fast as possible. Yes, I'll let you know. Second, in addition to the urgency of getting the passengers to hospital, there's now a very serious possibility that the plane will crash-land. I can't explain now but when the ship comes in she won't be under proper control." He listened for a moment to the man at the other end. "Yes, we've issued a general alarm. The fire department will have everything they've got standing by. The point is, I think the houses near the airport may be in some danger." He listened again. "Well, I'm glad you've suggested it. I know it's a hell of a thing to wake people in the middle of the night, but we're taking enough chances as it is. I can't guarantee at all that this plane will get down on the field. She's just as likely to pan down short or overshoot—that is, assuming she even gets this far. We're lucky that there are only those houses out towards Sea Island Bridge to worry about—they can be asked to stand by, can't they? We'll route her well clear of the city ... Eh? ... No, can't say yet. We'll probably try to bring her in from the east end of the main runway." Another pause, longer this time. "Thank you, Inspector. I realize that of course and I wouldn't make the request if I didn't regard this as a major emergency. I'll keep in touch." The controller clicked the telephone back, his face etched with worry. He asked the man at the radio panel, "Is 714 still standing by for us?" The dispatcher nodded. "This," remarked the controller to the room at large, "is going to be quite a night." He pulled out a handkerchief and wiped his face.

"The fire chief is on his way," reported his assistant. "I'm on to the Air Force now. They ask if they can give any assistance."

"We'll let them know, but I don't think so. Thank them." He returned to his study of the wall map, stuffing the handkerchief away in his pocket. Absently, his fingers probed an empty cigarette

76

pack, then tossed it on the floor in disgust. "Any-one got any smokes?"

"Here, sir."

He accepted a cigarette and lighted it. "You'd better send down for some—and coffee for every-one, too. We're going to need it."

Burdick came back into the room, breathing noisily. "Cross-Canada say their best man is Cap-tain Treleaven—they're ringing him now. He's at home and in bed, I suppose."

"I've arranged for a police escort if necessary."

"They'll take care of that. I've told them we need him in the worst way. Do you know Tre-leaven?"

"I've met him," said the controller. "He's a good type. We're lucky he's available."

"Let's hope he is," grunted Burdick. "We can certainly use him."

"What about the big brass?"

"I've put a call in to my president." He gri-maced.

The switchboard operator broke in. "I've got Seattle and Calgary waiting, sir. They want to know if we got the message from 714 clearly."

"Tell them yes," answered the controller. "Say we shall work the aircraft direct but we'd appreci-ate them keeping a listening watch in case we meet with any reception trouble."

"Right, sir."

The controller crossed to the radio panel and picked up the stand microphone. He nodded to the dispatcher who threw a switch to transmit.

"Vancouver Control to Flight 714," he called.

Spencer's voice, when he replied, spluttered from an amplifier extension high up in a corner of the room. Since his "mayday" distress call all his conversation had been channelled through the loudspeaker. "714 to Vancouver. I thought you were lost."

"Vancouver to 714. This is the controller speaking. We are organizing help. We shall call you again very soon. Meanwhile do nothing to interfere with the present set of the controls. Do you understand? Over."

Despite the distortion, the asperity in Spencer's voice came through like a knife. "714 to Vancouver. I thought I told you. I've never touched a job like this before. I certainly don't aim to start playing damn-fool tricks with the automatic pilot. Over."

The controller opened his mouth as if to say something, then changed his mind. He signed off and said to his assistant, "Tell Reception to get Treleaven up here as fast as hell when he arrives."

"Right, sir. The duty fire officer just checked back," reported the assistant. "He's clearing all runway vehicles and gas wagons well under cover before 714's ETA. The city's fire department is bringing all the equipment they've got into the precincts."

"Good. When the fire chief gets here, I want a word with him. If 714 reaches us, I don't want our own trucks moving out to her along the field. If we get her down at all, she's not likely to stay in one piece."

Burdick said suddenly, "Hey, with the city departments on to this, we'll have the press at any time." He tapped his teeth with a fat forefinger, appalled at the possibilities. "This will be the worst thing that ever happened to Maple Leaf," he went on quickly. "Imagine it—it'll be front page everywhere. Plane-load of people, many of them sick. No pilot. Maybe civilian evacuation from those houses out towards the bridge. Not to mention——"

The controller cut in, "You'd better let PR handle it from the start. Get Howard here, at the double. The board will know his home number." Burdick nodded to the switchboard operator, who ran his finger down an emergency list and then began to dial. "We can't duck the press on a thing like this, Harry. It's much too big. Cliff will know how to play it. Tell him to keep the papers off our backs. We've got work to do."

"What a night," Burdick groaned, picking up a telephone impatiently. "What happened to Dr. Davidson?" he demanded of the operator.

"Out on a night call and can't be reached. He's due back pretty soon. I've left a message."

"Wouldn't you know it? Everything has to happen tonight. If he doesn't check in in ten minutes, get the hospital. That doctor in 714 is maybe in need of advice. Come on, come on," Burdick breathed irritably into his telephone. "Wake up, Cliff, for Pete's sake. There's no reason why any one should sleep through this."

On the outskirts of the town another telephone was ringing incessantly, splitting the peacefulness of a small, neat house with its shrill clamor. A smooth white arm emerged from bedclothes, rested motionless across a pillow, then stirred again and groped slowly in the darkness for the switch of a bedside lamp. The lamp clicked on. With her eyes screwed up against the bright light, an attractive red-head in a white embroidered nightdress reached painfully for the telephone, then brought it to her ear and turned on her side. Peering at the hands of the little bedside clock, she mumbled, "Yes?"

"Is this Mrs. Treleaven?" demanded a crisp voice.

"Yes," she said, practically in a whisper. "Who is it?"

"Mrs. Treleaven, may I speak to your husband?"

"He's not here."

"Not there? Where can I find him, please? This is urgent."

She propped herself up on her pillow, trying to blink herself awake. The thought occurred to her that she was dreaming.

"Are you there?" asked the voice at the other end. "Mrs. Treleaven, we've been trying to reach you for several minutes."

"I took a sleeping pill," she said. "Look, who's calling at this time of night?"

"I'm sorry to wake you, but it's imperative that we contact Captain Treleaven without delay. This is Cross-Canada, at the airport."

"Oh." She gathered herself together. "He's at his mother's place. His father is ill and my husband is helping to sit with him."

"Is it in town?"

"Yes, not far from here." She gave the telephone number.

"Thank you. We'll ring him there."

"What's wrong?" she asked.

"I'm sorry—there isn't time to explain. Thank you again."

The line was dead. She replaced the receiver and swung her legs out of bed. As the wife of a senior pilot of an airline she was accustomed to unexpected duty calls on her husband, but although she had grown to accept them as an unavoidable part of his life, part of her still resented them. Was Paul the only pilot they ever thought of when they were in a fix? Well, if he was having to take over a plane in a hurry, he would need to call home first for his uniform and gear. There would be time to make up a flask of coffee and some sandwiches. She drew on a robe and stumbled sleepily out of the bedroom and down the stairs towards the kitchen.

Two miles away, Paul Treleaven slept deeply, his large frame stretched along the chesterfield in his mother's parlor. That determined and vigorous old lady had insisted on taking a spell by the side of her sick husband, ordering her son firmly to rest for a couple of hours while he could. The news from the family doctor the previous evening had been encouraging: the old man had passed the dangerous corner of his pneumonic fever and now it was a matter of careful nursing and attention. Treleaven had been thankful for the chance to sleep. Only thirty-six hours previously he had completed a flight from Tokyo, bringing back a parliamentary mission en route for Ottawa, and since then, with the crisis of his father's illness, there had been scant opportunity for more than an uneasy doze.

He was aroused by his arm being shaken. Immediately awake, he looked up to find his mother bending over him.

"All right, Mother," he said heavily, "I'll take over now."

"No, son, it isn't that. Dad's sleeping like a baby. It's the airport on the telephone. I told them you were trying to snatch some rest, but they insisted. I think it's disgraceful—just as if they can't wait until a respectable hour in the morning."

"Okay. I'll come."

Getting to his feet, he wondered if he were ever going to sleep properly again. He was already half-dressed, having removed only his jacket and tie so as to lie comfortably on the chesterfield. He padded in stockinged feet to the door and out to the telephone in the hall, his mother following anxiously behind him.

"Treleaven," he said.

"Paul, this is Jim Bryant." The words were clipped, urgent. "I was getting really worried. We need you, Paul, but bad. Can you come over right away?"

"Why, what's up?"

"We're in real trouble here. There's a Maple Leaf Charter—it's an Empress C6, one of the refitted jobs—on its way from Winnipeg with a number of passengers and both pilots seriously ill with food poisoning."

"What! *Both* pilots?"

"That's right. It's a top emergency. Some fellow is at the controls who hasn't flown for years. Fortunately the ship is on autopilot. Maple Leaf hasn't got a man here and we want you to come in and talk her down. Think you can do it?"

"Great Scott, I don't know. It's a tall order." Treleaven looked at his wrist watch. "What's the ETA?"

"05.05."

"But that's under two hours. We've got to move! Look, I'm on the south side of town——"

"What's your address?" Treleaven gave it. "We'll

have a police car pick you up in a few minutes. When you get here, go straight on up to the control room."

"Right. I'm on my way."

"And good luck, Paul."

"You're not kidding."

He dropped the phone and strode back to the parlor, pulling on his shoes without stopping to tie the laces. His mother held out his jacket for him.

"What is it, son?" she asked apprehensively.

"Trouble over at the airport, Mother. Bad trouble, I'm afraid. There's a police car coming to take me there."

"Police!"

"Now, now." He put an arm around her for a second. "It's nothing for you to worry about. But they need my help. I'll have to leave you for the rest of the night." He looked round for his pipe and tobacco and put them in his pocket. "Just a minute," he said, stopping in his tracks. "How did they know I was here?"

"I couldn't say. Perhaps they rang Dulcie first."

"Yes, that must be it. Would you give her a ring, Mother, and let her know everything is all right?"

"Of course I will. But what is the trouble about, Paul?"

"A pilot is sick on an aircraft due here soon. They want me to talk it down, if I can."

His mother looked puzzled. "What do you mean—talk it down?" she repeated. "If the pilot's sick, who's going to fly it?"

"I am, Mother—from the ground. Or I'm going to try to, anyway."

"I don't understand."

Maybe I don't either, Treleaven thought to himself five minutes later, seated in the back of a police car as it pulled away from the sidewalk and slammed viciously into top gear. Street lights flashed past them in ever quickening succession; the speedometer crept steadily round to seventy-five as the siren sliced into the night.

"Looks like a big night over at the field," remarked the police sergeant beside the driver, talking over his shoulder.

"So I gather," said Treleaven. "Can you fill me in on exactly what's happening?"

"Search me." The sergeant spat out of the window. "All I know is that every available car has been sent over to the airport to work from there in case the bridge estate has to be cleared. We were on our way there too until they stopped us and sent us back for you. I'd say they're expecting a hell of a bang."

"You know what?" interjected the young driver. "It's my guess there's a busted-up Stratojet coming in with a nuclear bombload."

"Do me a favor," said the sergeant with heavy scorn. "Your trouble is you read too many comics."

Never, Treleaven reflected grimly to himself, had he reached the airport so quickly. In no time, or so it seemed, they had reached Marpole and crossed Oak Bridge to Lulu Island. Then, bearing right, they crossed the river estuary again to Sea Island and past occasional police cruisers whose crews were already talking to bewildered house owners in doorways, until they were speeding along the last stretch of Airport Road, the lights of the long, low airport buildings beckoning them on. They braked suddenly, with a protesting screech of tires, to avoid a fire truck which was making a leisurely U-turn ahead of them. The sergeant swore, briefly but with feeling.

At the main reception building, Treleaven was out of the car, through the doors and had crossed the concourse before the wail of the siren died. Waving aside the commissionaire who hurried across to meet him, he made his way directly to the control room in the administration block. He could move remarkably fast for a man of his size. It was probably that loose-limbed agility which combined with a solidly built physique, lank fair hair and hard lean features, to make him an object of interest to many women. His features, angular and crooked, looked as if they had been inexpertly carved from a chunk of wood. Treleaven had a considerable reputation as a disciplinarian and more than one erring crew member had had cause to fear the cold light in those pale, almost watery-blue eyes.

He entered Control as Burdick was speaking anxiously and deferentially on the telephone.

". . . No, sir, he isn't qualified. He flew single-engine fighters in the war; nothing since . . . I've asked them that. This doctor on board says . . ."

The controller stepped quickly over to greet Treleaven. "I'm certainly glad to see you, Captain," he said.

Treleaven nodded towards Burdick. "Is that the fellow in the Empress he's talking about?" he asked.

"Yes. He's just got his president out of bed in Montreal. The old man sounds far from happy about it—and so am I. The call shouldn't have come in here. Hurry it up, Harry, will you?"

"What else can we do?" pleaded Burdick into the

telephone, sweating profusely. "We've got to talk him down. I've located Cross-Canada's chief pilot, Captain Treleaven—he just walked in the door now. We'll get on the radio with a check list and try to bring him in . . . We'll do the best we can, sir . . . Of course it's a terrible risk, but can you think of something better?"

Treleaven took from the dispatcher the clipboard of messages from 714 and read them carefully. With a quiet request, "Weather," he then consulted the latest meteorological reports. This done, he laid the papers down, raised his eyebrows somberly at the controller, and produced his pipe which he proceeded to fill. Burdick was still speaking.

". . . I've thought of that, sir. Howard will handle the press at this end—they aren't on to it yet . . . Yes, yes, we've suspended food service on all flights ex Winnipeg. That's all we know. I called you right away . . ."

"What do you think?" the controller asked Treleaven.

The pilot shrugged without answering and picked up the clipboard again. His face was set in deep lines as he read the messages again, drawing steadily on his pipe. A young man backed into the room, holding the door open with his leg as he maneuvered a tray bearing cardboard cartons of coffee. He handed a carton to the controller and set another down in front of Treleaven. The pilot ignored it.

". . . ETA is 05.05 Pacific Time," Burdick was saying with increasing exasperation. "I've a lot to do, sir . . . I'll have to get on with it . . . I'll call you

86

... I'll call you as soon as I know anything more
... Yes, yes ... G'bye." Putting down the telephone, he blew out his cheeks with relief. Turning
to Treleaven, he said, "Thank you very much for
coming, Captain. Have you got it all?"

Treleaven held up the clipboard. "This is the
whole story?"

"That's everything we know. Now I want you to
get on the horn and talk this guy down. You'll
have to let him get the feel of the airplane on the
way, you'll have to give him the landing check,
you'll have to talk him on to the approach, and—so
help me!—you'll have to talk him right down on to
the ground. Can you do it?"

"I can't perform a miracle," said Treleaven
evenly. "You know that the chances of a man who
has only flown fighter airplanes landing a four-
engine passenger ship are pretty slim, to say the
least?"

"Of course I know it!" Burdick exploded. "You
heard what I told Barnard. But do *you* have any
other ideas?"

"No," Treleaven said slowly, "I guess not. I just
wanted to be sure you knew what we were getting
into."

"Listen," shouted Burdick angrily. "There's a
ship full of people up there, some of them dying,
including the pilots. The biggest air disaster in
years, that's what we're getting into!"

"Keep your temper," said Treleaven coldly.
"We'll get nowhere fast by shouting." He glanced
down at the clipboard and then at the wall map.
"This is going to be very tough and a very long
shot," he said. "I want that fully understood."

"All right, gentlemen," said the controller. "You are perfectly right to emphasize the risk, Captain. We fully accept that."

"What choice is there?" Burdick demanded.

"Very well, then," said Treleaven. "Let's get started." He walked over to the radio operator. "Can you work 714 direct?"

"Yes, Captain. Reception's good. We can call them any time."

"Do it then."

The operator switched to transmit. "Flight 714. This is Vancouver. Do you read? Over."

"Yes, Vancouver," came Spencer's voice through the amplifier. "We hear you clearly. Go ahead, please."

The operator handed the stand microphone to Treleaven. "Okay, Captain. It's all yours."

"Am I on the air?"

"Go ahead now."

Holding the stand microphone in his hand, its cable trailing to the floor, Treleaven turned his back on the other men in the room. Legs braced apart, he stared unseeingly at a point on the wall map, his cold eyes distant in concentration. His voice, when he spoke, was steady and unhurried, easy with a confidence he did not feel. As he began, the other men visibly relaxed, as if his natural authority had temporarily relieved them of a crushing responsibility.

"Hullo, Flight 714," he said. "This is Vancouver. My name is Paul Treleaven and I'm a Cross-Canada Airlines captain. My job is to help you fly this airplane in. We shouldn't have too much trouble. I see that I'm talking to George Spencer. I'd

88

like to hear a little more about your flying experience, George."

Behind him, the flabby folds of Burdick's honest face had begun to shake in an uncontrollable spasm of nervous reaction.

SEVEN

0325—0420

SPENCER TENSED, shooting an involuntary glance at the girl in the seat beside him. Her eyes, in the greenish glow of the instrument panel, were fixed on his face. He looked away again, listening intently.

Treleaven was saying, "For instance, how many flying hours have you had? The message here says you've flown single-engine fighters. Have you had any experience at all of multi-engine planes? Let's hear from you, George."

Spencer's mouth was so dry when he replied that at first he could hardly speak. He cleared his throat.

"Hullo, Vancouver. 714 here. Glad to have you along, Captain. But let's not kid each other, please. I think we both know the situation. My flying up to now has been entirely on single-engine aircraft, Spitfires and Mustangs—I'd say about a thousand hours in all. But that was thirteen years ago. I've touched nothing since. Do you understand that? Over."

"Don't worry about that, George. It's like riding a bicycle—you never forget it. Stand by, will you?"

In the Vancouver Control, Treleaven pressed the cutout button on the arm of the microphone in his hand and looked at a slip of paper the controller held out for him to read.

"Try to get him on this course," said the controller. "The Air Force have just sent in a radar check." He paused. "Sounds pretty screwed up, doesn't he?"

"Yes—who wouldn't be, in his shoes?" Treleaven grimaced reflectively. "We've got to give him confidence," he said. "Without that there isn't a chance. Whatever happens, he mustn't lose his nerve. Keep it down, will you?" to the controller's assistant who was talking on the telephone. "If this guy doesn't hear me clearly he'll be in trouble fast and there will be nothing we can do about it." Then, to the dispatcher, "Okay. Make damn sure you don't lose them on the air." He released the cutout. "714. This is Treleaven. You are still on autopilot, right?"

"Yes, that's so, Captain," came the reply.

"All right, George. In a minute you can disengage the autopilot and get the feel of the controls. When you've had a bit of practice with them you are going to change your course a little. Listen very carefully, though, before you touch them. When you start handling the airplane the controls will seem very heavy and sluggish compared with a fighter. Don't let that worry you. It's quite normal. You've got a lot of airplane up there, so take it nice and steady. Watch your air speed all the time you are flying and don't let it fall below 120 knots while your wheels and flaps are up, otherwise you'll stall. I'll repeat that. Make absolutely sure at all times that your air speed doesn't fall below 120 knots. Now, one other thing. Do you have someone up there who can work the radio and leave you free for flying?"

"Yes, Vancouver. I have the stewardess here with me and she'll take over the radio now. It's all yours, Janet."

"Hullo, Vancouver. This is the stewardess, Janet Benson. Over."

"Why, it's you, Janet," said Treleaven. "I'd know that voice anywhere. You're going to talk to George for me, are you? Good. Now Janet, I want you to keep your eyes on that air-speed indicator. Remember that an airplane stays in the air because of its forward speed. If you let the speed drop too low, it stalls—and falls out of the air. Any time the ASI shows a reading near 120, you tell George instantly. Is that clear, Janet?"

"Yes, Captain. I understand."

"Back to you, George. Take this slowly and smoothly. I want you to unlock the autopilot—it's clearly marked on the control column—and take the airplane yourself, holding her straight and level. George, you watch the artificial horizon and keep the air speed steady. Climb and descent indicator should stay at zero. All right. Start now."

Spencer put his right forefinger over the autopilot release button on the control column. His face was rigid. Feet on the rudder bar and both arms ready, braced, he steeled himself for what might come.

"Tell him I'm switching over now," he told Janet. She repeated the message. His hand wavered for a moment on the button. Then, decisively, he pressed it hard. The aircraft swung a little to port but he corrected the tendency gently and she responded well enough to his feet on the rudder bar.

The vibration from the controls seemed to flow through his body like an electric current.

"Tell him okay," he gasped, his nerves taut as cables.

"714 here. We're flying straight and level." Janet's voice sounded miraculously sweet and calm to him.

"Well done, George. As soon as you've got the feel of her, try some very gentle turns, not more than two or three degrees. Can you see the turn indicator? It's almost directly in front of your eyes and slightly to the right, just by the panel-light shield. Over." Treleaven's eyes were closed with the effort of visualizing the cockpit layout. He opened them and spoke to the dispatcher. "Listen. I've got a lot of work to do with this man in the air, but we ought to start planning the approach and landing while there's plenty of time. Get the chief radar operator up here, will you, and let me talk to him."

Very gingerly Spencer extended his left leg and eased the control column over. This time it seemed an age before the aircraft responded to his touch and he saw the horizon indicator tilt. Gratified, he tried the other way; but now the movement was alarming. He looked down at the ASI and was shocked to see that it had dropped to 180 knots. Quickly he eased the control column forward. Then he breathed again as the speed rose slowly to 210. He would have to treat the controls with the utmost respect until he really understood the time lag; that was evident. Again he tried a shallow turn and pushed at the resisting weight of the rudder to hold it steady. Gradually he felt the ship answer. Then he straightened up, so as to keep approximately on the course they had been steering before.

Janet had lifted her eyes momentarily from the instrument panel to ask in a small voice, "How is it?"

Spencer tried to grin, without much success. The thought passed through his mind that this was rather like his days on the Link trainer all over again, only then nearly sixty lives did not hang in the balance and the instructor was not more than a few feet away in the same room. "Tell him I'm on manual and doing gentle turns, coming back on course each time," he said.

Janet gave the message.

"I should have asked you this before," came Treleaven's voice. "What kind of weather are you in up there?"

"It's clear where we are right now," answered Janet. "Except below us, of course."

"Uh-huh. You'd better keep me informed. Now, George, we have to press on. You may hit some cloud layer at any time, with a little turbulence. If you do, I want you to be ready for it. How does she handle?"

Spencer looked across to Janet. "Tell him—sluggish as hell, like a wet sponge," he said between clenched teeth.

"Hullo, Vancouver. As sluggish as a wet sponge," repeated Janet.

For a few brief seconds the tension at Vancouver Control eased and the group standing round the radio panel exchanged smiles.

"That's a natural feeling, George," said Treleaven, serious again, "because you were used to smaller airplanes. You'll have to expect it to feel even worse when you really throw her around up there, but you'll soon get used to it."

The dispatcher cut in, "I've the radar chief here."

"He'll have to wait," said Treleaven. "I'll talk to him as soon as I get a break."

"Right."

"Hullo, George," called Treleaven. "You must avoid any violent movements of the controls, such as you used to make in your fighter airplanes. If you *do* move the controls violently, you will over-correct and be in trouble. Is that understood? Over."

"Yes, Vancouver, we understand. Over."

"Now, George, I want you to try the effect of fore-and-aft control on your air speed. To start with, adjust your throttle setting so as to reduce speed to 160 and cruise straight and level. But watch the air speed closely. Keep it over 120. The elevator trim is just to your right on the control pedestal and the aileron trim is below the throttles, near the floor. Got it? Over."

Spencer checked with his hand, holding the plane steady with the other and with braced legs. "Right. Tell him I'm reducing speed."

"Okay, Vancouver, we're doing as you say."

Time ticked away as the speed slowly dropped. At 160 George adjusted the trim tabs and held up his thumb to Janet.

"714 here, Vancouver. 160 knots on the indicator."

Treleaven waited until he had struggled out of his jacket before speaking. "Right, George. Try a little up and down movement. Use the control column as carefully as if it were full of eggs and

95

watch the speed. Keep it at 160. Get the feel of the thing as you go along. Over." He put the microphone down. "Where's the radar chief?"

"Here."

"At what range will this aircraft show on your scope?" queried Treleaven.

"Sixty miles, thereabouts, Captain."

"That's no good for a while, then. Well," said Treleaven, partly to himself, partly to Burdick, "you can't have everything at once. I've had to assume that he's still heading in a general westerly direction. Next call, though, we'll check his heading."

"Yeah," said Burdick. He offered a cigarette, which the pilot refused.

"If he's stayed on the same heading," continued Treleaven, looking at the wall map, "he can't be that much off course, and we can straighten him up when he gets in our radar range. That Air Force check is a help."

"Can't he come in on the beam?" asked Burdick.

"Right now he's got enough to worry about. If I try to get him on the beam, he'll have to mess around with the radio, changing frequencies and a lot of other stuff. I'd sooner take a chance, Harry, and let him go a few miles off course."

"That makes sense," Burdick conceded.

"Here's how we'll handle it," said the pilot. He turned to the radar chief. "I'll do the talking. He's getting used to me now."

"Right, sir."

"As soon as he shows up on your scope, you can feed me the information and I'll relay it. Can you fix up a closed circuit between me and the radar room?"

"We can take care of that," said the dispatcher.

"How about the final approach?" asked the radar chief.

"We'll handle that the same way," said Treleaven. "Directly we've got him on the scope and he's steady on course, we'll move to the tower. You report up there and we'll decide on the runway and plan the approach."

"Yes, sir."

Treleaven picked up the microphone but waited, his eye catching that of the controller, who was replacing a telephone in its cradle.

"Dr. Davidson is downstairs," the controller told him.

"What does he have to say?"

"From the information we've got he agrees with the diagnosis of the doctor in the plane. Seemed to wonder at first if it could be an outbreak of botulism."

"What's that, for Pete's sake?"

"Some very serious kind of food poisoning, apparently. Shall we get the doctor up here and put him on the air?"

"No, Mr. Grimsell. It's more important right now to fly this airplane. We'll leave it to them to call for medical advice if they want it. I don't want Spencer's mind distracted from the job if I can possibly help it. I should have Davidson stand by in case he's needed." Treleaven spoke into the microphone. "Hullo, George Spencer. Don't forget that lag in the controls. Just take it steadily. Do you understand that?"

There was a pause. Then, "He understands, Vancouver. Over."

To Spencer it seemed as if the airline captain

must have read his thoughts. He had moved the column slowly forward, and then back again, but there had been no response from the aircraft. Now he tried again, easing the stick away from him. Imperceptibly at first, the nose of the aircraft began to dip. Then, so suddenly that he was momentarily paralyzed with shock, it plunged downwards. Janet bit hard on her lip to avoid screaming. The ASI needle began to swing round ... 180 ... 190 ... 200 ... 220. Putting all his weight on the column, Spencer fought to bring the aircraft back. In front of him the instrument panel seemed alive. The climb-and-descent indicator quivered against the bottom of the glass. The little facsimile of a plane on the artificial horizon had depressed its port wing and remained in that position, frighteningly. On the face of the altimeter the 100-foot hand whirred backwards; the 1,000-foot hand less quickly but still terrifyingly fast; while the 10,-000-foot needle had already stopped, jammed at its nadir.

"Come on, you slug, come on!" he shouted as the nose at last responded. He watched the three altimeter needles begin with agonizing slowness to wind up again, registering gradually increasing height. "Made it!" he said in relief to Janet, forgetting that he was overcorrecting.

"Watch it—watch the speed," she exclaimed.

His eyes flicked back to the dial, now rapidly falling again. 160 ... 150 ... 140. Then he had it. With a sigh the aircraft settled down on to an even keel once more and he brought it into straight and level flight.

"Jeeze, that was nasty," he muttered.

Janet was still checking the ASI. "160. That's all right now."

The door to the flight deck opened behind them and Dr. Baird's voice called, "What's wrong?"

Spencer answered loudly, not removing his eyes from the panel, "Sorry, Doc. I'm trying to get the feel of her."

"Well, take it as easy as you can, will you? Things are bad enough back here. How are you doing?"

"Fine, just fine, Doc," said Spencer, licking his lips. The door closed again and Treleaven's voice came on the air. "Hullo, George Spencer. Everything okay? Over."

"All under control, Vancouver," replied Janet.

"Good. What's your present heading, George?"

Spencer peered down. "Tell him the magnetic compass is still showing about 290 and I've been keeping fairly steady on that." She did so.

"Very well, George. Try to stay on that heading. You may be a little out, but I'll tell you when to correct. Right now I want you to feel how the ship handles at lower speeds when the flaps and wheels are down. But don't do anything until I give you the instructions. Is that clear? Over."

Janet got Spencer's nod and asked Treleaven to proceed.

"Hullo, 714. First of all, throttle back slightly, not much, and get your air speed steady at 160 knots. Adjust your trim to maintain level flight. Then tell me when you're ready. Over."

Spencer straightened himself and called over, "Watch that air speed, Janet. You'll have to call it off to me when we land, so you may as well start practicing now."

"It's on 190," Janet recited. "200 . . . 190 . . . He said 160, Mr. Spencer."

"I know, I know. I'm going to throttle back a bit."

He reached out for the throttles and eased them back. "What is it, Janet? What's the speed?"

"190, 180, 175, 170, 165, 155, 150 . . . That's too low!"

"I know. Watch it! Watch it!"

His hand nursed the throttle levers, almost caressing them into the exact positioning to achieve the speed he wanted. Janet's eyes were riveted on the flickering needle of the dial.

"150, 150, 155, 160 . . . it's steady on 160."

Spencer puffed out his cheeks. "Phew! That's got it. Tell him, Jan."

"Hullo, Vancouver. Our speed is steady on 160. Over."

Treleavan sounded impatient, as if he had expected them to be ready before this. "Okay, 714. Now, George. I want you to put on 15 degrees of flap, but be careful not to make it any more. The flap lever is at the base of the control pedestal and marked plainly: 15 degrees will mean moving the lever down to the second notch. The flap-indicator dial is in the center of the panel—the main panel. Have you got both of those? Can you see them? Over."

Spencer located the lever. "Confirm that," he told Janet, "but *you'd* better do it. Right?"

She acknowledged to Vancouver and sat waiting, her hand on the lever.

"Hullo, 714. When I tell you, push it all the way down and watch that dial. When the needle reaches 15 degrees, pull the lever up and leave it at the second notch. You'll have to watch and be ready for it. Those flaps come down in a hurry. All clear?"

"We're ready, Vancouver," said Janet.

"Right. Go ahead, then."

She prepared to depress the lever, then jerked her head up in alarm.

"The air speed! It's down to 125."

Spencer's eyes flicked over to the air-speed indicator. Then desperately he pushed the control column forward. "Call it off!" he roared. "Call it off!"

The lurch of the aircraft brought their stomachs to their mouths. Janet almost crouched in front of the panel, intoning the figures.

"135, 140, 150, 160, 170, 175 . . . Can't you get it back to 160?"

"I'm trying, I'm trying." Again he levelled off and jockeyed the controls until the ASI had been coaxed back to the reading required. He passed his sleeve hurriedly over his forehead, afraid to remove his hand from the column for long enough to get out a handkerchief. "There it is. 160, isn't it?"

"Yes, that's better."

"That was close." He sat back in his seat. "Look, let's relax for a minute, after that." He managed to muster up a smile. "You can see the kind of pilot I am. I should have known that would happen."

"No, it was my job to watch the air speed." She took a deep breath to steady her pounding heart. "I think you're doing wonderfully," she said. Her voice shook slightly.

It was not lost on Spencer. He said quickly and with exaggerated heartiness, "You can't say I didn't warn you. Come on, then, Janet. Let's get going."

"Hullo, George," Treleaven's voice crackled in the earphones. "Are your flaps down yet?"

"We're just about to put them down, Captain," said Janet.

"Hold it. I omitted to tell you that when the flaps are down you will lose speed. Bring it back to 140. Over."

"Well, I'll be—!" Spencer ejaculated. "That's mighty nice of him. He cut it pretty fine."

"It's probably hectic down there," said Janet, who had a very good idea of the scene taking place at the airport. "Thank you, Captain," she said, transmitting. "We're starting now. Over." At a nod from Spencer she pushed the lever down as far as it would go, while Spencer watched the indicator carefully.

"Right. Now back to second notch."

With infinite caution he cajoled the ASI needle until it rested steadily at 140.

"Tell him, Janet."

"Hullo, Vancouver. Our flaps are down 15 degrees and the air speed is 140."

"714. Are you still maintaining level flight?"

Spencer nodded to her. "Tell him, yes—well, more or less, anyway."

"Hullo, Vancouver. More or less."

"Okay, 714. Now the next thing is to put the wheels down. Then you'll get the feel of the airplane as it will be when you're landing. Try to keep your altitude steady and your speed at 140. When you are ready—and make sure you *are* ready —put down the landing gear and let the speed come back to 120. You will probably have to advance your throttle setting to maintain that air speed, and also adjust the trim. Is that understood? Tell me if you are doubtful about anything. Over."

"Ask him," said Spencer, "what about propeller controls and mixture?"

At Janet's question, Treleaven said in an aside to Burdick, "Well, this guy's thinking, anyway. For the time being," he said into the microphone, "leave them alone. Just concentrate on holding that air speed steady with the wheels and flaps down. Later on I'll give you a full cockpit check for landing. Over."

"Tell him, understood," said Spencer. "We're putting down the wheels now." He looked apprehensively at the selector lever by his leg. It seemed a much better idea to keep both hands on the column. "Look, Janet, I think you'd better work the undercart lever and call off the air speed as the wheels come down."

Janet complied. The arrest in their forward flight was so pronounced that it was like applying a brake, jerking them in their seats.

"130, 125, 120, 115 . . . It's too low."

"Keep calling!"

"115, 120, 120 . . . Steady on 120."

"I'll get this thing yet," Spencer panted. "She's like the Queen Mary."

Treleaven's voice came up, with a hint of anxiety. "All okay, George? Your wheels should be down by now."

"Wheels down, Vancouver."

"Look for three green lights to show you that they're locked. Also there's a pressure gauge on the extreme left of the center panel, and the needle should be in the green range. Check."

"Are they on?" asked Spencer. Janet looked and nodded. "Better tell him, then."

"Yes, Vancouver. All correct."

"And say she still handles like a wet sponge, only more so."

"Hullo, Vancouver. The pilot says she still handles like a sponge, only more so."

"Don't worry about that. Now we'll put on full flaps, shall we, and then you'll have the proper feel of the aircraft on landing. You'll soon get the hang of it. Now follow me closely. Put full flap on, bring your air speed back to 110 knots and trim to hold you steady. Adjust the throttle to maintain the altitude. Then I'll give you instructions for holding your height and air speed while you raise the landing gear and flaps. Over."

"Did you say 110, Captain?" Janet queried nervously.

"110 is correct, Janet. Follow me exactly and you'll have nothing to worry about. Are you quite clear, George?"

"Tell him, yes. We are putting on full flap now."

Once more her hand pushed hard on the flap lever and the air speed started to fall.

"120, 115, 115, 110, 110 . . ."

Spencer's voice was tight with the effort of will he was imposing on himself. "All right, Janet. Let him know. By God, she's a ton weight."

"Hullo, Vancouver. Flaps are full on and the air speed is 110. Mr. Spencer says she is heavier than ever."

"Nice going, George. We'll make an airline pilot of you yet. Now we'll get you back to where you were and then run through the procedure again, with certain variations regarding props, mixture, boosters, and so on. Okay? Over."

"Again!" Spencer groaned. "I don't know if I can take it. All right, Janet."

"Okay, Vancouver. We're ready."

"Right, 714. Using the reverse procedure, adjust your flaps to read 15 degrees and speed 120 knots. You will have to throttle back slightly to keep that speed. Go ahead."

Reaching down, Janet grasped the flap lever and gave it a tug. It failed to move. She bent closer and tried again.

"What is it?" asked Spencer.

"Sort of stiff. I can't seem to move it this time."

"Shouldn't be. Give it a good steady pull."

"It must be me. I just can't make it budge."

"Here. Let me." He took his hand off the column and pulled the lever back effortlessly. "There, you see. You've got to have the touch. Now if you'll just rest it in the second——"

"Look out!" she screamed. "The air speed!"

It was 90, moving to 75.

Bracing himself against the sudden acute angle of the flight deck, Spencer knew they were in a bad stall, an incipient spin. Keep your head, he ordered himself savagely—*think*. If she spins, we're finished. Which way is the stall? It's to the left. Try to remember what they taught you at flying school. Stick forward and hard opposite rudder. *Stick forward*. Keep it forward. We're gaining speed. Opposite rudder. Now! Watch the instruments. They can't be right—I can feel us turning! No—trust them. You must trust them. Be ready to straighten. That's it. Come on. Come on, lady, *come on*.

"The mountains!" exclaimed Janet. "I can see the ground!"

Ease back. Ease back. Not too fast. Hold the air speed steady. We're coming out ... we're coming out! It worked! It worked! We're coming out!

"105, 110, 115 ..." Janet read off in a strangled tone. "It's completely black now. We must be in fog or something."

"Get the wheels up!"

"The mountains! We must——"

"Get the wheels up, I said!"

The door to the flight deck crashed open. There were sounds of crying and angry voices.

"What are they doing?" came a yell from a woman.

"There's something wrong! I'm going to find out what it is!"

"Get back to your seat." This was Baird's voice.

"Let me through!"

The silhouette of a man filled the doorway, peering into the darkness of the flight deck. He lurched forward, grabbing hold of anything to keep himself upright, and stared in petrified disbelief at the back of Spencer's head and then down at the prostrate figures of the two men on the floor. For a moment his mouth worked soundlessly. Then he impelled himself back to the open doorway and gripped the jamb on both sides as he leaned through it.

His voice was a shriek.

"He's not the pilot! We shall all be killed! We're going to crash!"

EIGHT

WREATHED IN woolly haloes, the neon lights at the entrance to the reception building at Vancouver Airport glistened back from the wet driveway. Usually quiet at this pre-dawn hour of the night, except for the periodic arrival or departure of an airport coach, the wide sweep of asphalt now presented a very different scene. At the turnoff from the main highway into the airport approach on the mainland side of the river, a police cruiser stood angled partly across the road, its roof light blinking a constant warning. Those cars which had been allowed through along Airport Road were promptly waved by a patrolman to parking spaces well clear of the entrance to Reception. Some of their occupants remained out in the damp night air for a while, talking in low voices and stamping the ground occasionally to keep warm, in order to watch the arrival from time to time of fire rigs and ambulances as they halted for a few seconds to receive directions to their assembly points. A gleaming red salvage truck engaged gear and roared away, and in the small pool of silence immediately following its noise the sound of a car radio carried clearly across for several yards.

"Ladies and gentlemen, here is a late bulletin

from Vancouver Airport. The authorities here stress that although the Maple Leaf Airline flight is being brought in by an inexperienced pilot, there is no cause for alarm or panic in the city. All precautions are being taken to warn residents in the airport area and at this moment emergency help is streaming out to Sea Island. Stay with this station for further announcements."

A mud-streaked Chevrolet braked harshly at the reception building, swung over to the parking lot, its tires squealing viciously on the asphalt, and stopped abruptly. On the lefthand side of its windscreen was pasted a red sticker, PRESS. A big man, thickset with graying hair, and wearing an open trench coat, got out and slammed the door. He walked rapidly over to Reception, nodded to the patrolman and hurried inside. Dodging two interns in white medical coats, he looked round for the Maple Leaf Airline desk and made his way over to it quickly. Two men stood there in discussion with a uniformed staff member of the airline, and at the touch of the big man one of them turned, smiling briefly in greeting.

"What's the score, Terry?" asked the big man.

"I've given the office what I've got, Mr. Jessup," said the other man, who was very much younger. "This is Ralph Jessup—Canadian International News," he added to the passenger agent.

"Who's handling it here?" asked Jessup.

"I think Mr. Howard is about to make a statement in the press room," said the passenger agent.

"Let's go," said Jessup. He took the younger man by the arm and drew him away. "Is the office sending up a camera team?" he asked.

"Yes, but there'll be a pretty full coverage by

everyone. Even the newsreels may make it in time."

"H'm. Remind the office to cover the possible evacuation of houses over near the bridge. The same man can stay on the boundary of the field. If he climbs the fence he may get one or two lucky shots of the crash—and get away quicker than the others. What about this guy who is flying the plane?"

"A George Spencer of Toronto. That's all we know."

"Well, the office will get our Toronto people on to that end. Now grab a pay booth in Reception here and don't budge out of it, whatever happens. Keep the line open to the office."

"Yes, Mr. Jessup, but——"

"I know, I know," said Jessup sadly, "but that's the way it is. If there's a foul-up on the phones in the press room, we'll need that extra line."

His coat flapping behind him, he strode across the concourse, head down like an angry bull, out of Reception and along to the press room. There several newsmen were already foregathered, three of them talking together, another rattling at one of the six or eight typewriters on the large center table, and a further couple using two of the telephone booths that lined two sides of the paneled room. On the floor were dumped leather cases of camera equipment.

"Well," said Jessup sardonically, "what kept you boys?"

"Hi, Jess," greeted one of the men. "Where's Howard? Have you seen him?"

"On his way, I'm told." Jessup shook himself out a cigarette. "Well, who knows what?"

"We just got here," said Stephens of the *Monitor*. "I put a call in to the controller's office and got blasted."

"You fellows have it easy on this one," Jessup remarked, lighting his cigarette and spitting out a shred of tobacco. "It's too late for the mornings and in plenty of time for the evenings, unless you put out special midmorning runs. It's easy to see who's doing the work." He indicated the two men in the telephone cubicles, one from CP and the other UPA.

"Wrap it up, Jess," said Stephens. "To listen to you wire service fellers, you'd think——"

"Quit horsing around," cut in Abrahams of the *Post-Telegram*. "We'd better start shouting up for some action. Pretty soon all the others'll be here and we won't be able to move."

They turned as a youngish man entered, holding in his hand some slips of paper. This was Cliff Howard, high-spirited and energetic, whose crew-cut hair, rimless spectacles and quietly-patterned English neckties were a familiar and popular sight at the airport. He did not smile at the newsmen, although most of them were personal friends of his.

"Thanks for staying put," he told them.

"We very nearly didn't," returned Stephens. The two agency men had hurriedly terminated their calls and joined the others.

"Let's have it, Cliff," said one of them.

Howard looked at Jessup. "I see you've come straight from bed like me, Jess," he remarked, nodding at the pajamas under Jessup's jacket.

"Yes," said Jessup shortly. "Come on, Cliff. Snap it up."

Howard glanced down at the papers in his hand,

then back at the men gathered round him. There was a film of perspiration on his forehead. "All right," he said. "Here it is. A Maple Leaf Empress was chartered in Toronto to bring supporters to the ball game today. On the Winnipeg leg to here both the pilot and the copilot have been taken ill. A passenger is at the controls. He hasn't had experience of this type of airplane before. We're talking him down—Captain Paul Treleaven, Cross-Canada's chief pilot, is on the job—but the authorities thought it advisable to take precautionary measures in clearing the area and bringing in extra help in case of accident."

There was a pause. "Well?" growled one of the newsmen.

"I guess there's not much more I can tell you," said Howard apologetically. "We're doing all we can and I'd sure appreciate it if——"

"For God's sake, Cliff, what are you giving us?" protested Stephens. "How does it happen *both* the pilots are ill?"

Howard shrugged uncomfortably. "We don't yet know for sure. It may be some kind of stomach attack. We have doctors standing by——"

"Now listen," Jessup interrupted tersely. "This is no time to play the innocent, Cliff. There have been enough leaks on this story already to sink a ship. Everything you've just said, our offices knew before we got here. Let's start again. What's the truth about the rumor of food poisoning?"

"Who is the guy who's piloting the ship?" added Abrahams.

Howard breathed deeply. He smiled and made a dramatic gesture of flipping notes to the floor. "Look, boys," he said expansively, "I'll lay it on the line for you—you know I never hold back from you if I can help it. But if I stick my neck out I know you'll play along with me. That's fair, isn't it? We don't want to get the thing out of perspective. What's happening tonight is a big emergency— why should I pretend it isn't?—but everything that's humanly possible is being done to minimize the risk. The whole operation reflects the greatest credit on the airport organization. Frankly, I've never seen anything——"

"The story, Howard!"

"Sure, sure. But I want you to understand that nothing I say can be taken as an official statement, either on behalf of the airport or the Maple Leaf Airline. The airline is very properly giving all their attention to getting the plane down safely, and I'm just filling in to help you boys along." A telephone shrilled, but no one made a move towards it. "All right, then," said Howard. "So far as my information goes, there has been an outbreak of sickness on the plane which may very possibly be food poisoning. Of course we are taking——"

"Do you mean," someone interposed, "that the food on board the plane was contaminated?"

"No one can answer that question yet. All I can tell you is this, and I want you to get it straight. Fog delayed the departure of the Empress from Toronto and it was late on arrival at Winnipeg—so late that the normal caterers were not available. Food was obtained from another firm instead. Some of that food was fish, and some of that fish, gentlemen, may, I repeat may, have been contaminated. The usual procedure is being carried out by the public health authorities in Winnipeg."

"What about the guy who's taken over?" repeated Abrahams.

"Please understand," continued Howard, "that the Maple Leaf Airline has the very strictest standards of hygiene. An accident like this is a million-to-one freak that could happen despite the most stringent——"

"The guy at the wheel! Who is he?"

"One at a time," said Howard shrewdly, as if warding off a barrage of questions. "The plane's crew is one of Maple Leaf's most experienced teams—as you know, that's saying a lot. Captain Lee Dunning, First Officer Peter Levinson and Stewardess Janet Benson—I've got full details right here——"

"Save that," said Jessup. "We'll pick it up later." Two more newsmen hurried into the room and pushed into the group. "What's the story on the passenger who's flying the crate?"

"My information is that the first officer, then the captain were taken sick. Luckily there was a passenger on board who had piloted before and he took over the controls with the most remarkable smoothness. Name of George Spencer, from Winnipeg, I assume—he joined the plane there."

"When you say he has flown before," persisted Abrahams, "do you mean he's an ex-airline pilot?"

"Well, no," admitted Howard. "I believe he flew extensively in the war in smaller aircraft——"

"In the war? That was years ago."

"What kind of smaller aircraft?" Jessup demanded.

"Spitfires, Mustangs, quite a wide range of——"

"Hold it. Those were fighters. Is this man a fighter pilot from the war?"

113

"Flying is flying, after all," Howard insisted anxiously. "He's under radio tuition from Captain Paul Treleaven, Cross-Canada's chief pilot, who will talk him down."

"But hell," said Jessup almost disbelievingly, "the Empress is a four-engine job. What's its horsepower?"

"Oh, around 8,000, I'd say."

"And you mean that an ex-wartime pilot who was used to single-engine fighters can handle after all these years a multi-engine airliner?" There was a scramble as two or three of the newsmen broke away to the telephone booths.

"Naturally there is some risk," Howard conceded, "which is why the precaution has been taken of clearing the immediate vicinity. The situation is pretty tight, I freely admit, but there's no reason to——"

"Some risk!" echoed Jessup. "I've done a little flying myself—I can imagine what that guy is going through. Let's have more about him."

Howard spread his hands. "I know nothing more about him than that."

"What!" exclaimed Stephens. "That's all you know about someone who's trying to bring in a shipload of—how many people *are* on board?"

"Fifty-nine, I believe, including the crew. I've got a copy of the passenger list for you, if you'll just——"

"Cliff," said Jessup grimly, "if you hole up on this one . . ."

"I've told you, Jess, that's all I have on him. We all wish we knew more, but we don't. He seems to be doing well, on the last report."

"How long have we got before the crash?" Abrahams pressed.

Howard jerked round to him. "Don't assume that," he retorted. "She's due in round about an hour, maybe less."

"Are you beaming her in?"

"I'm not sure, but I think Captain Treleaven intends to talk her down. Everything is fully under control. The airlanes and the field have been cleared. The city fire department is moving in extra help, just in case."

"Suppose she overshoots into the water?"

"That's not likely, but the police have alerted every available launch to stand by. I've never known such complete precautions."

"Wow, what a story!" Abrahams shouted and dived into the nearest booth, keeping the door open while he dialed so that he could continue to listen.

"Cliff," said Jessup, with some sympathy for the public relations man, "how long will the gas last in this ship?"

"I can't say, but there's bound to be a safety margin," answered Howard, loosening his tie. He sounded far from convinced.

Jessup looked at him for a second or two with narrowed eyes. Then it struck him. "Wait a minute," he shot out. "If there's food poisoning on board, it can't be only the pilots who've gone down with it?"

"I'll need all the help you can send," Abrahams was saying into the telephone. "I'll give it to you as I get it. When you've got enough to close for the first run, you'd better pull it up both ways—for the crash, and for miracle landing—and hold it. Okay?

Switch me to Bert. Bert, you ready? Starts. 'At dawn this morning Vancouver Airport witnessed the worst——' "

"Look, Jess," said Howard urgently, "this is dynamite. You can have it all the way, but for pity's sake play it fair to the people upstairs. They're working like crazy. There's nothing that could help the people in that aircraft that isn't being done."

"You know us all here, Cliff. We won't cross you up. What *is* the condition of those passengers?"

"A number of them are ill, but there's a doctor on board who is giving what treatment he can. We have further medical advice available on the radio if required. The stewardess is okay and she's helping Spencer, relaying the messages. You've got the lot now."

"Food poisoning is a mighty serious thing," Jessup pursued relentlessly. "I mean, the time factor is everything."

"That's so."

"If those people don't get down pretty damn soon, they could even—die?"

"That's about it," Howard agreed, tight-lipped.

"But—but this is a world story! What's the position up there now?"

"Well, about ten, fifteen minutes ago——"

"That's no good!" Jessup roared. "A few minutes can change the whole situation in a thing like this. Get the position now, Cliff. Who's duty controller tonight? Ring him—or I will, if you like."

"No, not for a while, Jess, please. I tell you they're——"

Jessup gripped the public relations man by the shoulder. "You've been a newspaperman, Cliff. Either way this will be the biggest air story for years, and you know it. In an hour's time you'll have a tiger on your back—this place will be stiff with reporters, newsreels, TV, the lot. You've got to help us now, unless you want us busting out all over the airport. Get us the exact present position and you can take a breather for a few minutes while we get our stories through."

"Okay, okay. Ease off, will you?" Howard picked up an internal telephone from the table. "This is Howard. Control Room, please." He pulled down his lower lip at Jessup. "You'll get me crucified. Hullo, Control? Is Burdick there? Put me on, it's urgent. Hullo, Harry? Cliff. The press are crowding up, Harry. I can't hold them much longer. They want the full situation as of now. They've got deadlines to meet."

"Of course!" snorted Burdick sarcastically in the control room. "Certainly! We'll arrange for the flight to crash before their deadlines. Anything for the newspapers!"

"Take it easy, Harry," urged Howard. "These guys are doing their job."

Burdick lowered the telephone and said to the controller, who was standing with Treleaven before the radio panel, "Mr. Grimsell. Things are boiling up a bit for Cliff Howard. I don't want to leave here. Do you think Stan could take a few minutes out to talk to the press?"

"I think so," answered the controller. He looked over to his assistant. "What about it? We'd better keep those boys under control. You could make it fast."

"Sure, sir. I'll do that."

"No point in holding back," Burdick advised.

"Tell 'em the whole thing—up to and excluding this," and he nodded to the radio panel.

"I get it. Leave it to me." The assistant left the room.

"The assistant controller is coming down, Cliff," said Burdick and rang off. He heaved his bulk over to the two men at the radio panel, mopping his face with a crumpled handkerchief. "Are you getting anything?" he asked in a flat voice.

Treleaven shook his head. He did not turn. His face was gray with fatigue. "No," he said dully. "They've gone."

The controller rapped to the switchboard operator, "Teletype Calgary and Seattle, priority. Find out if they're still receiving 714."

"714, 714. Vancouver Control to 714. Come in, 714," called the radio operator steadily into the microphone.

Treleaven leaned against the radio desk. The pipe in his hand was dead. "Well," he said wearily, "this could be the end of the line."

"714, 714. Do you hear me? Come in, please."

"I can't take much more," said Burdick. "Here, Johnnie," to one of the clerks, "get some more coffee, for the love of Mike. Black and strong."

"Hold it!" exclaimed the radio operator.

"Did you get something?" asked the controller eagerly.

"I don't know ... I thought for a minute...." Bending close to the panel, his headset on, the operator made minute adjustments to his fine tuning controls. "Hullo, 714, 714, this is Vancouver." He called over his shoulder, "I can hear *something* ... it may be them. I can't be sure. If it is, they're off frequency."

"We'll have to take a chance," said Treleaven. "Tell them to change frequency."

"Flight 714," called the operator. "This is Vancouver. This is Vancouver. Change your frequency to 128.3 Do you hear that? Frequency 128.3."

Treleaven turned to the controller. "Better ask the Air Force for another radar check," he suggested. "They should be on our own scope soon."

"714. Change to frequency 128.3 and come in," the operator was repeating.

Burdick plumped back on to a corner of the center table. His hand left a moist mark on the woodwork. "This can't happen—it can't," he protested in a gravel voice to the whole room, staring at the radio panel. "If we've lost them now, they'll fry—every last manjack of them."

NINE

0435—0505

LIKE A MAN in a nightmare, possessed with the fury
of desperation, his teeth clenched and face
streaked with sweat, Spencer fought to regain control of the aircraft, one hand on the throttle lever
and the other gripped tightly on the wheel. Within
him, oddly at variance with the strong sense of
unreality, he felt scorching anger and self-disgust.
Somewhere along the line, and quickly, he had not
only lost altitude but practically all his air speed
too. His brain refused to go back over the events of
the last two minutes. Something had happened to
distract him, that was all he could remember. Or
was that an excuse too? He couldn't have lost so
much height in just a few seconds; they must have
been steadily descending before that. Yet it was
surely not long since he had checked the climb-
and-descent indicator—or wasn't that its function?
Could it be the gas——?

He felt a violent, almost uncontrollable desire to
scream. Scream like a child. To scramble out and
away from the controls, the ironically flickering
needles and the mocking battery of gauges, and
abandon everything. Run back into the warm,
friendly-lit body of the aircraft crying out, *I
couldn't do it. I told you I couldn't do it and you*

120

wouldn't listen to me. No man should be asked to do it——

"We're gaining height," came Janet's voice, incredibly level now it seemed. He remembered her with a shock and in that moment the screaming in his mind became the screams of a woman in the passenger compartment behind him—wild, maniacal screams.

He heard a man shouting, "He's not the pilot, I tell you! They're stretched out there, both of them. We're done for!"

"Shut up and sit down!" rasped Baird clearly.

"You can't order me about——"

"I said get back! Sit down!"

"All right, Doctor," came the adenoidal tones of 'Otpot, the man from Lancashire, "just leave him to me. Now, you——"

Spencer shut his eyes for an instant in an effort to clear the dancing of the illuminated dials. He was, he realized bitterly, hopelessly out of condition. A man could spend his life rushing from this place to that, forever on the go and telling himself he could never keep it up if he wasn't absolutely fit. Yet the first time a real crisis came along, the first time that real demands were made of his body, he fell flat on his face. That was the most savage thing of all: to know that your body could go no further, like an old car about to run backwards down a hill.

"I'm sorry," said Janet.

Still maintaining his pressure on the column, he shot a glance of complete surprise at her.

"What?" he said stupidly.

The girl half twisted in her seat towards him. In the greenish light from the instrument panel, her pale face looked almost translucent.

"I'm sorry for giving way like that," she said simply. "It's bad enough for you. I—I couldn't help it."

"Don't know what you're talking about," he told her roughly. He didn't know what to say. He could hear the woman passenger, sobbing loudly now. He felt very ashamed.

"Trying to get the bus up as fast as I can," he said. "Daren't do more than a gentle climb or we'll lose way again."

Baird's voice called from the doorway, above the rising thunder of the engines, "What *is* going on, anyway, in there? Are you all right?"

Spencer answered, "Sorry, Doc. I just couldn't hold her. I think it's okay now."

"Try to keep level, at least," Baird complained. "There are people very, very ill back here."

"It was my fault," said Janet. She saw Baird sway with exhaustion and hold on to the door jamb to steady himself.

"No, no," protested Spencer. "If it hadn't been for her we'd have crashed. I just can't handle this thing—that's all there is to it."

"Rubbish," said Baird curtly. They heard a man shout, "Get on the radio!" and the doctor's voice raised loudly to address the passengers, "Now listen to me, all of you. Panic is the most infectious disease of the lot, and the most lethal too." Then the door slammed shut, cutting him off.

"That's a good idea," said Janet calmly. "I ought to be reporting to Captain Treleaven."

"Yes," agreed Spencer. "Tell him what's happened and that I'm regaining height."

Janet pressed her microphone button to transmit and called Vancouver. For the first time there was no immediate acknowledgment in reply. She called again. There was nothing.

Spencer felt the familiar stab of fear. He forced himself to control it. "What's wrong?" he asked her. "Are you sure you're on the air?"

"Yes—I think so."

"Blow into your mike. If it's alive you'll hear yourself."

She did so. "Yes, I heard all right. Hullo, Vancouver. Hullo, Vancouver. This is 714. Can you hear me? Over."

Silence.

"Hullo, Vancouver. This is 714. Please answer. Over."

Still silence.

"Let me," said Spencer. He took his right hand from the throttle and depressed his microphone button. "Hullo, Vancouver. Hullo, Vancouver. This is Spencer, 714. Emergency, emergency. Come in, please."

The silence seemed as solid and as tangible as a wall. It was as if they were the only people in the world.

"I'm getting a reading on the transmitting dial," said Spencer. "I'm sure we're sending okay." He tried again, with no result. "Calling all stations. Mayday, mayday, mayday. This is Flight 714, in serious trouble. Come in anybody. Over." The ether seemed completely dead. "That settles it. We must be off frequency."

"How could that have happened?"

"Don't ask me. *Anything* can happen, the way we were just now. You'll have to go round the dial, Janet."

"Isn't that risky—to change our frequency?"

"It's my guess it's already changed. All I know is that without the radio I might as well put her nose down right now and get it over. I don't know where we are, and even if I did I certainly couldn't land in one piece."

Janet slid out of her seat, trailing the cord from her headset behind her, and reached up to the radio panel. She clicked the channel selector round slowly. There was a succession of crackles and splutters.

"I've been right the way round," she said.

"Keep at it," Spencer told her. "You've got to get something. If we have to, we'll call on each channel in turn." There was a sudden, faraway voice. "Wait, what's that!" Janet clicked back hurriedly. "Give it more volume!"

". . . to 128.3," said the voice with startling nearness. "Vancouver Control to Flight 714. Change to frequency 128.3. Reply please. Over."

"Keep it there," said Spencer to the girl. "Is that the setting? Thank our lucky stars for that. Better acknowledge it, quick."

Janet climbed back into her seat and called rapidly, "Hullo, Vancouver, 714 answering. Receiving you loud and clear. Over."

With no perceptible pause Vancouver came back, the voice of the dispatcher charged with eagerness and relief.

"714. This is Vancouver. We lost you. What happened? Over."

"Vancouver, are we glad to hear you!" said Janet, holding her forehead. "We had some trouble. The airplane stalled and the radio went off. But it's all right now—except for the passengers, they're not taking it any too well. We're climbing again. Over."

This time it was Treleaven speaking again, in the same confident and measured manner as before but clearly with immense thankfulness. "Hullo, Janet. I'm glad you had the good sense to realize you were off frequency. George, I warned you about the danger of a stall. You must watch your air speed all the time. There's one thing: if you've stalled and recovered, you obviously haven't lost your touch as a pilot."

"Did you get that?" Spencer asked Janet unbelievingly. They exchanged nervously strained smiles.

Treleaven was continuing: "You've probably had a bit of a scare, so we'll take it easy for a minute or two. While you're getting some height under you I want you to give me some readings from the instrument panel. We'll start with the fuel-tank gauges . . ."

While the captain recited the information he wanted, the door to the passenger deck opened and Baird looked in again, about to call to the two figures forward. He took in their concentration on the instrument panel and checked himself. Then he entered, closing the door behind him, and dropped on one knee beside the forms of the pilot and first officer, using his ophthalmoscope as a flashlight to examine their faces. Dun had rolled partly out of his blankets and was lying with his knees drawn up, moaning softly. Pete appeared to be unconscious.

The doctor readjusted the covers, wrapping them in tightly. He mopped the men's faces with a damp hand towel stuffed in his pocket and remained crouched in thought for a few seconds. Then he rose, bracing himself against the tilt of the deck. Janet was relaying figures into her microphone. Without a word the doctor let himself out, carefully sliding the door closed.

The scene outside resembled a vast casualty ambulance rather than the passenger deck of an airliner. At intervals along the crowded cabin, their reclining seats fully extended, sick passengers lay swaddled in rugs. One or two were quite motionless, scarcely breathing. Others were twisting in pain while friends or relatives watched them fearfully or replaced damp cloths on their foreheads.

Bending forward, the more effectively to render his homily to the man he had recently thrust back into his seat, 'Otpot was saying, "I don't blame you, see. 'Appen it's better sometimes to let off steam. But it don't do to start shouting in front of the others who're poorly, especially the ladies. Old Doc here is real champion and so are the two up front flying. Any road, we've got to trust them, see, if we want to get down at all."

Temporarily subdued, the passenger, who was twice the size of 'Otpot, stared stonily at his own reflection in the cabin window by his seat. The perky little Englishman came along to the doctor, who patted his arm in thanks.

"You're quite a wizard, aren't you?" said Baird.

"I'm more scared than he is," 'Otpot assured him fervently, "and that's a fact. Heck, if you hadn't been with us, Doctor. . . ." He shrugged expressively. "What d'you make of things now?" he asked.

"I don't know," Baird replied. His face was gaunt. "They had a little trouble up front. It's hardly surprising. I think Spencer is under a terrible strain. He's carrying more responsibility than any of us."

"How much longer is there to go?"

"I've no idea. I've lost all sense of time. But if we're on course it can't be long now. Feels like days to me."

'Otpot put to him as quietly as he could, "What d'you really think, Doc? 'Ave we got a chance?"

Baird shook the question off in tired irritation. "Why ask me? There's always a *chance,* I suppose. But keeping an airplane in the air and getting it down without smashing it to a million pieces, with all the factors that involves, are two mighty different propositions. I guess that much is obvious even to me. Either way, it isn't going to make much odds to some of the folk here before long."

He squatted down to look at Mrs. Childer, feeling inside her blanket for her wrist and noting her pinched, immobile face, dry skin, and quick, shallow breathing. Her husband demanded hoarsely, "Doctor, is there *nothing* we can do for her?"

Baird looked at the closed, sunken eyes of the woman. He said slowly, "Mr. Childer, you've a right to know the truth. You're a sensible man—I'll give it to you straight. We're making all the speed we possibly can, but at best it will be touch and go for your wife." Childer's mouth moved wordlessly. "You'd better understand this," Baird went on deliberately. "I've done what I could for her, and I'll continue to do it, but it's pathetically little. Earlier on, using morphia, I might have been able to ease the pain for your wife. Now, if it's any consolation to you, nature has taken care of it for us."

Childer found his voice. "I won't have you say

that," he protested. "Whatever happens, I'm grateful to you, Doctor."

"Of course he is," interposed 'Otpot heartily. "We all are. No one could've done owt more than you, Doc. An absolute marvel, that's what."

Baird smiled faintly, his hand on the woman's forehead. "Kind words don't alter the case," he said harshly. "You're a man of courage, Mr. Childer, and you have my respect. But don't delude yourself." The moment of truth, he thought bitterly; so this is it. I'd known it was coming tonight, and I knew too, deep down, what the answer would be. This is the salty taste of the real truth. No romantic heroics now. No colored-up and chlorophylled projection of what you *think* you are, or what you like others to think you are. This is the truth. Inside another hour we shall all very probably be dead. At least I shall go exposed for what I am. A rotten, stinking failure. *When the time came, he was unequal.* The perfect obituary.

"I'm telling you," Childer was saying with emotion, "if we get out of this, I'll have everyone know what we owe to you."

Baird collected his thoughts. "What's that?" he grunted. "I'd give plenty to have two or three saline drips aboard." He rose. "Carry on as before, Mr. Childer. Make sure she's really warm. Keep her lips moistened. If you can get her to take a little water now and then, so much the better. Remember she's lost a very critical amount of body fluids."

At that moment, in the control room at Vancouver, Harry Burdick was in the process of replacing some of his own body fluid with another carton of coffee. In addition to the microphone held in his hand, Treleaven now had on a headset and into the latter he was asking, "Radar. Are you getting anything at all?"

From another part of the building the chief radar operator, seated with an assistant before a long-range azimuth scanner, answered in a calmly conversational tone, "Not a thing yet."

"I can't understand it," Treleaven said to the controller. "They ought to be in range by now."

Burdick volunteered, "Don't forget he lost speed in that last practice."

"Yes, that's so," Treleaven agreed. Into his headset he said, "Radar, let me know the instant you get something." To the controller, "I daren't bring him down through cloud without knowing where he is. Ask the Air Force for another check, will you, Mr. Grimsell?" He nodded to the radio operator. "Put me on the air. Hullo, 714. Now, listen carefully, George. We are going through that drill again but before we start I want to explain a few things you may have forgotten or that only apply to big airplanes. Are you with me? Over."

Janet replied, "Go ahead, Vancouver. We are listening carefully. Over."

"Right, 714. Now before you can land certain checks and adjustments must be carried out. They are in addition to the landing drill you've just practiced. I'll tell you when and how to do them later. Now I just want to run over them to prepare you. First, the hydraulic booster pump must be switched on. Then the brake pressure must be showing about 900 to 1,000 pounds a square inch. You'll maybe remember something along these lines from your fighter planes, but a refresher course won't hurt. Next, after the wheels are down you'll turn on the fuel booster pumps and check that the gas feed is sufficient. Lastly, the mixture has to be made good and rich and the propellers set. Got all that? We'll take it step by step as you come in so that Janet can set the switches. Now I'm going to tell you where each of them are. Here we go. . . ."

Janet and Spencer identified each control as they were directed.

"Tell him we have them pinpointed, Janet."

"Hullo, Vancouver. We're okay on that."

"Right, 714. You're in no doubt about the position of each of those controls, Janet? You're quite sure? Over."

"Yes, Vancouver. I've got them. Over."

"714. Check again that you are in level flight. Over."

"Hullo, Vancouver. Yes, flying level now and above cloud."

"Right, 714. Now, George. Let's have 15 degrees of flap again, speed 140, and we'll go through the wheel-lowering routine. Watch that air speed like a hawk this time. If you're ready, let's go. . . ."

Grimly Spencer began the procedure, following each instruction with complete concentration while Janet anxiously counted off the air speed and operated the flap and undercarriage levers. Once again they felt the sharp jolt as their speed was arrested. The first tentative streaks of dawn were glimmering to eastward.

In the control room, Treleaven took the opportunity to gulp some cold coffee. He accepted a cigarette from Burdick and exhaled the smoke noisily. He looked haggard, with a blue stubble around his chin.

"How do you read the situation now?" queried the airline manager.

"It's as well as can be expected," said the captain, "but time's running dangerously short. He should have at least a dozen runs through this flap and wheels drill alone. With luck we'll get about three in before he's overhead—that is, if he's on course."

"You're going to give him practice approaches?" put in the controller.

"I must. Without at least two or three I wouldn't give a red cent for his chances, not with the experience he's got. I'll see how he shapes up. Otherwise. . . ." Treleaven hesitated.

Burdick dropped his cigarette to the floor and stepped on it. "Otherwise what?" he prompted.

Treleaven rounded on them. "Well, we'd better face facts," he said. "That man up there is frightened out of his wits, and with good reason. If his nerve doesn't hold, they may stand more chance by ditching offshore in the ocean."

"But—the impact!" Burdick exclaimed. "And the sick people—and the aircraft. It'd be a total loss."

"It would be a calculated risk," said Treleaven icily, looking the rotund manager straight in the eyes. "If our friend looks like piling up all over the field, your airplane will be a write-off anyway."

"Harry didn't mean it like that," broke in the controller hurriedly.

"Hell, no, I guess not," said Burdick uncomfortably.

"With the added danger," continued Treleaven, "that if he crashes here, fire is almost certain and we'll be lucky to save anyone. He may even take some ground installation with him. Whereas if he puts down on the ocean he'll break up the airplane, sure, but we stand a chance of saving some of the passengers if not the very sick ones. With this light mist and practically no wind the water will be pretty calm, reducing the impact. We'd belly-land him by radar as near as we could to rescue craft."

"Get the Navy," the controller ordered his assistant. "Air Force too. Air-sea rescue are already standing by. Have them put out offshore and await radio instructions."

"I don't want to do it," said Treleaven, turning back to the wall map. "It would amount to abandoning the sick passengers. We'd be lucky to get them out before the plane went under. But it may be necessary." He spoke into his headset. "Radar, are you getting anything?"

"Still nothing," Came the even, impersonal reply. "Hold it, though. Wait a minute. This may be something coming up.... Yes, Captain. I have him now. He's ten miles south of track. Have him turn right on to a heading of 265."

"Nice work," said Treleaven. He nodded to be put on the air as the switchboard operator called across, "Air Force report visual contact, sir. ETA 38 minutes."

"Right." He raised the microphone in front of him. "Hullo, 714. Have you carried out the reverse procedure for flaps and undercart? Over."

"Yes, Vancouver. Over," came the girl's voice.

"Any trouble this time? Flying straight and level?"

"Everything all right, Vancouver. The pilot says— so far." They heard her give a nervous little laugh.

"That's fine, 714. We have you on radar now.

You're off course ten miles to the south. I want you to bank carefully to the right, using your throttles to maintain your present speed, and place the aircraft on a heading of 265. I'll repeat that. 265. Is that clear? Over."

"Understood, Vancouver."

Treleaven glanced out of the window. The darkness outside had lightened very slightly. "At least they'll be able to see a little," he said, "though not until the last minutes."

"I'll put everything on stand-by," said the controller. He called to his assistant, "Warn the tower, Stan. Tell them to alert the fire people." Then, to the switchboard operator, "Give me the city police."

"And then put me on to Howard in the press room," added Burdick. He said to Treleaven, "We'd better explain to those guys about the possibility of ditching before they start jumping to their own conclusions. No, wait!" He suddenly remembered, staring intently at the captain. "We can't admit that would mean writing off the sick passengers. I'd be cutting my throat!"

Treleaven was not listening. He had slumped into a chair, his head bowed with a hand over his eyes, not hearing the confused murmur of voices about him. But at the first splutter as the amplifier came alive he was on his feet, reaching for the microphone.

"Hullo, Vancouver," called Janet. "We are now on a heading of 265 as instructed. Over."

"714. That's fine," said Treleaven with an assumed cheerfulness. "You're doing splendidly. Let's have it all again, shall we? This will be the last time before you reach the airport, George, so make it good."

The controller was speaking with quiet urgency into his telephone. "Yes, they'll be with us in about a half hour. Let's get the show on the road."

TEN

0505—0525

SPENCER TRIED to ease his aching legs. His whole body felt pummeled and bruised. In his anxiety and the effort of concentration he had expended almost unnecessary energy, leaving him, the moment he relaxed, utterly drained of strength. He was conscious of his hands trembling and made no attempt to check them. As he watched the unceasing movement of the instruments, a fleck of light rose constantly in front of his eyes, slowly falling again like a twist of cotton. All the time that interior voice, now every bit as real to him and as independent as the one in his earphones, kept up its insistent monologue, telling him: *Whatever you do, don't let go. If you let go, you're finished. Remember, it was like this many a time in the war. You thought you'd reached the end then— completely bushed, with not another ounce left in you. But every time there was something left in the bag—one last reserve you never knew you had.*

He looked across to Janet, willing himself to speak. "How did we make out that time?" he asked her. He knew he was very near to collapse.

She seemed to sense the purpose of his question. "We did pretty well," she said brightly. "Anyway, I

135

thought Captain Treleaven sounded pleased, didn't you?"

"Hardly heard him," he said, turning his head from side to side to relieve the muscles in his neck. "I just hope that's the lot. How many times have we done the flap and wheel routine now—is it three? If he asks us to do it once more, I'll ..." *Steady on,* he admonished himself. *Don't let her see what a state you're in.* She had leaned over to him and wiped his face and forehead with a handkerchief. *Come on now, get a grip. This is only nervous reaction—blue funk, if you like. Think of Treleaven: what a spot he's in. He's safe on the ground, sure enough, but suppose he forgot something——*

"Have you noticed, the sun's coming up," said Janet.

"Why sure," he lied, lifting his eyes. Even ahead to the west the carpet of cloud was tinged with pink and gold, and there too the vast canopy of sky had perceptibly lightened. To the south, on the port beam, he could see two mountain tops, isolated like islands in a tumbling ocean of cotton wool. "We won't be long now." He paused.

"Janet."

"Yes?"

"Before we go down, have a last—I mean, another look at the pilots. We'll probably bump a bit—you know—and we don't want them thrown about."

Janet flashed a grateful smile at him.

"Can you hold on there for a moment?" she asked.

"Don't worry, I'll yell quick enough."

She slipped off her headset and rose from her

seat. As she turned to get out, the door to the passenger deck opened and Baird looked in.

"Oh—you're off the radio," he observed.

"I was just going to have a look at the captain and copilot, to make sure they're secure."

"No need to," he told her. "I did it a few minutes ago, when you were busy."

"Doctor," called Spencer, "how are things with you back there?"

"That's why I looked in," said Baird tersely. "We're running out of time—but fast."

"Is there any kind of help that we can get you on the radio?"

"I'd liked to have had a diagnostic check with a doctor down there, but I guess it's more important to hold the air open for flying the machine. How long is it likely to be now?"

"Well under the half hour, I'd say. How does that sound?"

"I don't know," Baird said doubtfully. He held on to the back of Spencer's seat, weariness apparent in every inch of his posture. He was in shirt sleeves, his tie discarded. "There are two patients in a state of complete prostration," he went on. "How much longer they can last without treatment, I can't say. But not long, that's for sure. And there are several others who'll soon be just as bad, unless I'm very wrong."

Spencer grimaced. "Is anyone giving you a hand?"

"You bet—couldn't possibly manage, otherwise. One feller in particular—that English character—he's really turned out a——"

The earphones came to life. "Hullo, 714. This is Vancouver. Over."

Spencer waved Janet back into her seat and she hurriedly donned her headset.

"Well, I'll get back," said Baird. "Good luck, anyway."

"Wait a minute," said Spencer, nodding to the girl.

"714 here," Janet acknowledged into her microphone. "We'll be with you in a moment."

"Doctor," said Spencer, speaking quickly, "I don't have to fool you. This may be rough. Just about anything in the book is liable to happen." The doctor said nothing. "You know what I mean. They may get a bit jumpy back there. See that they're kept in their seats, huh?"

Baird seemed to be turning words over in his mind. Then he replied in a gruff tone, "Do the best you can and leave me to take care of the rest." He thumped the young man lightly on the shoulder and made his way aft.

"Okay," said Spencer to the girl.

"Go ahead, Vancouver," she called.

"Hullo, 714," responded the clear, confident voice of Treleaven. "Now that you've had a breather since that last run-through, George, we'd better press on again. You should be receiving me well now. Will you check, please? Over."

"Tell him I've been having a few minutes with my feet up," said Spencer. "And tell him he's coming in about strength niner." *Strength niner,* he thought. *You really dug that one up.*

". . . a short rest," Janet was saying, "and we hear you strength niner."

"That's the way, George. Our flying practice has slowed you down a bit, though that's all to the good as it will be getting light when you come in.

You are now in the holding position and ready to start losing height. First I want to speak to Janet. Are you listening, Janet?"

"Hullo, Vancouver. Yes, I hear you."

"Janet, when we make this landing we want you to follow the emergency crash procedures for protection of passengers. Do you understand? Over."

"I understand, Captain. Over."

"One more thing, Janet. Just before the landing we will ask the pilot to sound the emergency bell. And, George—the switch for that bell is right over the copilot's seat and it's painted red."

"Can you see it?" asked Spencer without looking up.

"Yes," said Janet, "it's here."

"All right. Remember it."

"Janet," continued Treleaven, "that will be your warning for final precautions, because I want you to be back then with the passengers."

"Tell him no," Spencer cut in. "I must have you up front."

"Hullo, Vancouver," said Janet. "I understand your instructions, but the pilot needs me to help him. Over."

There was a long pause. Then, "All right, 714," Treleaven answered. "I appreciate the position. But it is your duty, Janet, to see that all emergency crash precautions are taken before we can think about landing. Is there anyone you can explain and delegate this to?"

"What about the doctor?" suggested Spencer.

Janet shook her head. "He's got enough on his plate," she said.

"Well, he'll have a bit more," he snapped. "I've

139

got to have you here if we're to stand any chance of getting down."

She hesitated, then pressed the stud to transmit. "Hullo, Vancouver. Dr. Baird will in any case have to keep a watch on the sick passengers as we land. I think he's the best person to carry out the emergency drill. There's another man who can help him. Over."

"Hullo, Janet. Very well. Detach yourself now and explain the procedure very carefully to the doctor. There must be no possibility of error. Let me know when you're through." Janet laid aside her headset and climbed out of her seat. "Now George," Treleaven went on, "watch that you keep to your present course: I'll give you any corrections as necessary. Right now, as you approach the airport, I'll give you a cockpit check of the really essential things. I want you to familiarize yourself with them as we go along. Some of them you'll remember from your old flying days. Be certain you know where they are. If you're in any doubt this is the time to say so. We'll have as many dummy runs as you like but when you do finally come in the procedure must be carried out properly and completely. We'll start on the first check directly Janet gets back on the air."

In the control room at Vancouver, Treleaven took a dead cigarette from his mouth and tossed it away. He looked up at the electric wall clock and back at the controller. "How much gas have they got?" he demanded.

Grimsell picked up the clipboard from the table. "In flying time, enough for about ninety minutes," he said.

"What's the angle, Captain?" asked Burdick.

"You figure there's plenty of time for circuits and approaches, don't you?"

"There's got to be," said Treleaven. "This is a first-flight solo. But keep a strict check on it, will you, Mr. Grimsell? We must have plenty in hand for a long run-in over the ocean, if I decide as a last measure to ditch."

"Mr. Burdick," hailed the switchboard operator, "your president is on the line."

Burdick swore. "At this time, he has to get back! Tell him I can't speak to him now. Put him through to the Maple Leaf office. Wait a minute. Put me on to the office first." He picked up a telephone and waited impatiently. "Is that you, Dave? Harry. Surprise for you—the Old Man is on the line. Hold him off as best you can. Tell him 714 is in holding position and his prayers are as good as ours. I'll ring him directly the—directly I have something to tell him. Then I suppose he'll jump a plane here. Right, boy."

The assistant to the controller, his hand cupped over a telephone, was saying to his chief, "It's Howard. He says the press are——"

"I'll take it." The controller seized the telephone. "Listen, Cliff. We're accepting no more non-operational calls. Things are far too critical now. . . . Yes, I know. If they've got eyes, they'll see for themselves." He replaced the receiver with a bang.

"I'd say that boy was doing a pretty good job," grunted Burdick.

"He is, too," agreed the controller. "And those newspapermen wouldn't be doing *their* job by keeping quiet. But we can't be distracted now."

Treleaven stood by the radio panel, his fingers

drumming absently, his eyes fixed on the clock. Outside the airport, in the first light of dawn, the emergency measures were in full swing. At a hospital a nurse hung up her telephone and spoke to a doctor working at an adjacent table. She handed him his coat, reaching also for her own. They hurried out and a few minutes later the overhead door to the vehicle bay of the hospital slid up, emitting first one ambulance and then another.

In a city fire hall one of the few crews to be held to the last minute on reserve slapped down their cards and raced for the door at the sound of the bell, snatching up their clothing equipment on the way. The last man out skidded back to the table and lifted up the cards of one of his opponents. He raised an eyebrow, then dived after his colleagues.

At the little group of houses near Sea Island Bridge, which lay in direct line with the airfield, police were shepherding families into two buses, most of the people with street clothes thrown hastily over their night attire. A small girl, staring intently at the sky, tripped over her pajamas. She was picked up instantly by a policeman and deposited in a bus. He waved to the driver to get started.

"Hullo, Vancouver," called Janet, a little breathlessly. "I've given the necessary instructions. Over."

"Good girl," said Treleaven with relief. "Now, George," he went on quickly, "the clock is running a little against us. First, reset your altimeter to 30.1. Then throttle back slightly, but hold your air speed steady until you're losing height at 500 feet per minute. Watch your instruments closely. You'll have a long descent through cloud."

Spencer spread his fingers round the throttles

and gently moved them back. The climb-and-descent indicator fell slowly and a little unevenly to 600, then rose again to remain fairly steady at 500.

"Here comes the cloud," he said, as the gleams of daylight were abruptly blotted out. "Ask him how high the cloud base is below."

Janet repeated the question.

"Ceiling is around 2,000 feet," said Treleaven, "and you should break out of cloud about fifteen miles from the airport."

"Tell him we're holding steady at 500 feet a minute," instructed Spencer.

Janet did so.

"Right, 714. Now, George, this is a little more tricky. Don't break your concentration. Keep a constant check on that descent indicator. But at the same time, if you can, I want you to pinpoint the controls in a first run-through of landing procedure. Think you can manage that?"

Spencer did not trouble to answer. His eyes rooted on the instrument panel, he just set his lips and nodded expressively.

"Yes, Vancouver," said Janet. "We'll try."

"Okay, then. If anything gets out of hand, tell me immediately." Treleaven shook off a hand someone had laid on his arm to interrupt him. His eyes were screwed up tightly as he looked again at the blank spot on the wall, visualizing there the cockpit of the aircraft. "George, this is what you will do as you come in. First, switch the hydraulic booster pump *on*. Remember, just fix these things in your mind—don't do anything now. The gauge is on the extreme left of the panel, under and to the left of the gyro control. Got it? Over."

He heard Janet's voice reply, "The pilot knows that one, Vancouver, and has located the switch,"

"Right, 714. Surprising how it comes back, isn't it, George?" Treleaven pulled out a handkerchief and wiped the back of his neck. "Next you'll have to turn off the de-icer control. That's bound to be on and will show on the gauge on the right of the panel, just in front of Janet. The flow control is next to it. That one's easy, but the control must be off before you land. Watching the descent indicator, George? Next item, brake pressure. There are two gauges, one for the inboard brake and one for the outboard. They're immediately to the right of the hydraulic boost which you've just found. Over."

After a pause, Janet confirmed, "Found them, Vancouver. They're showing 950 and—er—1,010 pounds—is it per square inch?—each."

"Then they're okay, but they must be checked again before landing. Now, the gills. They must be one-third closed. The switch is right by Janet's left knee and you'll see it's marked in thirds. Are you with me? Over."

"Yes, I see it, Vancouver. Over."

"You can work that one, Janet. Next to it, on the same bank of switches, are the port and starboard intercooler switches. They're clearly marked. They will have to be opened fully. Make sure of that, Janet, won't you? Open fully. The next and most important thing is the landing gear. You've been through the drill, but go over it thoroughly in your mind first, starting with the flap movement and ending with the wheels fully down and locked. Full flap should be put on when the plane is very near touch-down and you're sure you're going to come in. I shall direct you on that. Is this understood by both of you? Over."

"Tell him yes, thanks," said Spencer, his eyes not leaving the panel. His shoulder had begun to itch abominably, but he blanked his mind to the irritation.

"Okay, 714. When you're on the approach, and after the wheels are down, the fuel booster pumps must be turned on. Otherwise your supply of gas might be cut off at the worst moment. The switch for these is at five o'clock from the autopilot, just behind the mixture controls."

Janet scanned the panel in a daze. *"Where?"* she almost whispered to Spencer. He peered at the board and located the switch. "There." His finger stabbed at the little switch, above the grooved bank that held the throttle levers.

"All right, Vancouver," she said weakly.

"Now the mixture is to be changed to auto rich. I know George has been itching for that, so I won't say any more—he'll handle that all right. Then you have to set the propellers until the green lights under the switches come on. They're just about touching George's right knee, I should think. Got them?"

"Pilot says yes, Vancouver."

"Lastly, the superchargers. After the wheels are down, these must be set in the take-off position— that is, up, on your aircraft. They are, of course, the four levers to the left of the throttles. Well, now. Any questions about all that? Over."

Spencer looked at Janet despairingly. "It's all one big question," he said. "We'll never remember it all."

"Hullo, Vancouver," said Janet. "We don't think we'll be able to remember it."

"You don't have to, 714. I'll remember it for you. There are some other points, too, which we'll deal with when we come to them. I want to go over these operations with you thoroughly, George, so that when I give the word you'll carry out the action without too much loss of concentration. Remember, this is just a drill in flipping over switches. You still have to fly the aircraft."

"Ask him about time," said Spencer. "How much have we got?"

Janet put the question to Vancouver.

"As I said, George, you've got all the time in the world—but we just don't want to waste any. You'll be over the airport in about twelve minutes. Don't let that bother you. There'll be as much time as you like for further practice." A pause. "'Radar reports a course adjustment necessary, George. Change your heading five degrees to 260, please. Over."

Treleaven switched off his microphone and spoke to the controller. "They're well on the glide path now," he said. "As soon as we've got visual contact, I'll level them off and take them around for circuits and drills. We'll see how they shape up after that."

"Everything's set here," said the controller. He called to his assistant, "Put the entire field on alert."

"Hullo, Vancouver," came Janet's voice over the amplifier. "We have now changed course to 260. Over."

"Okay, 714." Treleaven hitched up his trousers with one hand. "Let's have a check on your height, please. Over."

146

"Vancouver," answered Janet after a few seconds, "our height is 2,500 feet."

On his headset, Treleaven heard the radar operator report, "Fifteen miles from the field." "That's fine, George," he said. "You'll be coming out of cloud any minute. As soon as you do, look for the airport beacon. Over."

"Bad news," Burdick told him. "The weather's thickening. It's starting to rain again."

"Can't help that now," rapped Treleaven. "Get the tower," he told the controller. "Tell them to light up—put on everything they've got. We'll be going up there in a minute. I'll want their radio on the same frequency as this. Spencer won't have time to fool around changing channels."

"Right!" said the controller, lifting a telephone.

"Hullo, 714," Treleaven called. "You are now fifteen miles from the airport. Are you still in cloud, George? Over."

A long pause followed. Suddenly the radio crackled into life, catching Janet in mid-sentence. She was saying excitedly, ". . . lifting very slightly. I thought I saw something. I'm not sure. . . . Yes, there it is! I see it! Do you see it, Mr. Spencer? It's right ahead. We can see the beacon, Vancouver!"

"They've broken through!" Treleaven shouted it. "All right, George," he called into the microphone, "level off now at 2,000 feet and wait for instructions. I'm moving to the control tower now, so you won't hear from me for a few minutes. We'll decide on the runway to use at the last minute, so you can land into wind. Before that you'll make some dummy runs, to practice your landing approaches. Over."

They heard Spencer's voice say, "I'll take this,

Janet." There was a broken snatch of conversation, then Spencer came on the air again, biting off his words.

"No dice, Vancouver. The situation up here doesn't allow. We're coming straight in."

"What!" shouted Burdick. "He can't!"

"Don't be a fool, George," said Treleaven urgently. "You've *got* to have some practice runs."

"I'm holding my line of descent," Spencer intoned deliberately, his voice shaking slightly. "There are people up here dying. Dying! Can you get that into your heads? I'll stand as much chance on the first run-in as I will on the tenth. I'm coming straight in."

"Let me talk to him," appealed the controller.

"No," said Treleaven, "there's no time for argument." His face was white. A vein in his temple pulsed. "We've got to act fast. I say we've no choice. By all the rules he's in command of that airplane. I'm going to accept his decision."

"You can't do that," Burdick protested. "Don't you realize——"

"All right, George," Treleaven called, "if that's the way you want it. Stand by and level off. We're going to the tower now. Good luck to us all. Listening out." He ripped off his headset, flinging it down, and shouted to the others, "Let's go." The three men leaped out of the room and raced along the corridor, Burdick bringing up the rear. Ignoring the elevator, they bounded up the stairs, almost knocking over a janitor, coming down, and burst into the tower control room. An operator stood at the massive sweep of window, studying the lightening sky through night binoculars. "There he is!" he announced. Treleaven snatched up a

148

second pair of glasses, took a quick look, then put them down.

"All right," he said, panting. "Let's make our decision on the runway."

"Zero-eight," said the operator. "It's the longest and it's pretty well into the wind."

"Radar!" called the captain.

"Here, sir."

Treleaven crossed to a side table on which appeared a plan of the airport under glass. He used a thick chinagraph pencil to mark the proposed course of the aircraft.

"Here's what we do. Right now he's about here. We'll turn him so he begins to make a wide left-hand circuit, and at the same time bring him down to a thousand feet. I'll start the pre-landing check here, then we'll take him over the sea and make a slow turn around on to final. That clear?"

"Yes, Captain," said the operator.

Treleaven took a headset that was handed to him and put in on. "Is this hooked up to the radar room?" he asked.

"Yes, sir. Right here."

The controller was reciting into a telephone-type microphone: "Tower to all emergency vehicles. Runway is two-four. Two-four. Airport tenders take positions numbers one and two. Civilian equipment number three. All ambulances to positions numbers four and five. I repeat that no vehicle will leave its position until the aircraft has passed it. Start now."

Leaning down on the top of a control console, the captain flicked the switch of a desk microphone. At his elbow the spools of a tape recorder began to revolve.

149

"Hullo, George Spencer," he called in a steady, even tone. "This is Paul Treleaven in Vancouver tower. Do you read me? Over."

Janet's voice filled the control room. "Yes, Captain. You are loud and clear. Over."

Over the telephone, the calm voice of the radar operator reported, "Ten miles. Turn to a heading of 253."

"All right, George. You are now ten miles from the airport. Turn to a heading of 253. Throttle back and begin to lose height to one thousand feet. Janet, put the preliminary landing procedure in hand for the passengers. Neither of you acknowledge any further transmissions unless you wish to ask a question."

Removing his hands one at a time from the control column, Spencer flexed his fingers. He managed a grin at the girl beside him. "Okay, Janet, do your stuff," he told her.

She unhooked a microphone from the cabin wall and pressed the stud, speaking into it. "Attention please, everyone. Attention please." Her voice cracked. She gripped the microphone hard and cleared her throat. "Will you please resume your seats and fasten your safety belts. We shall be landing in a few minutes. Thank you."

"Well done," Spencer complimented her. "Just like any old landing, eh?"

She tried to smile back, biting her lower lip. "Well, not quite that," she said.

"You've got plenty of what it takes," said Spencer soberly. "I'd like you to know I couldn't have held on this far without. . . ." He broke off, gently moving the rudder and the ailerons, waiting to feel the response from the aircraft. "Janet," he

150

said, his eyes on the instruments, "we haven't much more time. This is what we knew must happen sooner or later. But I want to make sure you understand why I must try to get her down—somehow—on the first shot."

"Yes," she said quietly, "I understand." She had clipped her safety belt around her waist and now her hands were clenched together tightly in her lap.

"Well, I want to say thanks," he went on, stumblingly. "I made no promises, right from the start, and I make none now. You know, if anyone does, just how lousy I am at this. But taking turns around the field won't help. And some of the folk in the back are getting worse every minute. Better for them to . . . to take their chance quickly."

"I told you," she said. "You don't have to explain."

He shot a look of alarm at her, afraid in the passing of a moment that he stood exposed to her. She was watching the air-speed indicator; he could not see her face. He glanced away, back along the broad stretch of wing behind them. It was describing with infinite slowness the tiny segment of an arc, balancing on its tip the misty blue-gray outline of a hillside twinkling with road lamps. Sliding under the body of the aircraft, on the other quarter, were the distantly blazing lights of the airport. They seemed pathetically small and far away, like a child's carelessly discarded string of red and amber beads.

He could feel his heart thumping as his body made its own emergency preparations, as if aware that what remained of its life could now be measured in minutes, even seconds. He looked critical-

151

ly at himself, a man apart, performing the movements to bring the aircraft back to level flight.

He heard himself say, "Here we go, then. This is it, Janet. I'm starting to lose height—*now*."

ELEVEN

HARRY BURDICK lowered his binoculars and handed them back to the tower controller.

From the observation balcony which girdled the tower, the two men took a last look over the field, at the gasoline tankers pulled well back from the apron and, clearly visible now in the half-light, the groups of figures watching from the boarding bays. The steady throb of truck engines from the far end of the field seemed to add to the oppressive, almost unbearable air of expectancy which enveloped the whole airport.

Searching in his mind for any possible fault, Burdick reviewed Treleaven's plan. The aircraft would arrive overhead at something below two thousand feet and carry on out over the Strait of Georgia, descending gradually on this long, down-wind leg while the last cockpit check was executed. Then would follow a wide about-turn on to the final approach, giving the pilot maximum time in which to regulate his descent and settle down carefully for the run-in.

A good plan, one which would take advantage too of the slowly increasing light of dawn. It occurred to Burdick what that would mean to those of the passengers who were well enough to care.

They would watch Sea Island and the airport pass beneath them, followed by the wide sweep of the bay, then the island getting shakily nearer again as their emergency pilot made his last adjustments to the controls. Burdick sensed, as if he were up there with them, the suffocating tension, the dreadful choking knowledge that they might well be staring death in the face. He shivered suddenly. In his sweat-soaked shirt, without a jacket, he felt the chill of the early-morning air like a knife.

There was the sensation, quickly passing, of being suspended in time, as if the world were holding its breath.

"We are on a heading of 253." The girl's voice carried to them distinctly from the radio amplifier. "We are now losing height rapidly."

His eyes shadowed with anxiety, Burdick glanced meaningly into the face of the young man at his side. Without a word they turned and re-entered the great glass surround of the control tower. Treleaven and Grimsell were crouched before the desk microphone, their features bathed in the glow from the runway light indicators set into the control console in front of them.

"Wind still okay?" asked the captain.

Grimsell nodded. "Slightly across runway zero-eight, but that's still our best bet." Zero-eight was the longest of the airport's three runways, as Treleaven well knew.

"Radar," said Treleaven into his headset, "keep me fed the whole time, whether or not you can hear that I'm on the air. This won't be a normal talk-down. Scrap procedure the instant 714 runs into trouble. Cut in and yell."

Burdick tapped him on the shoulder. "Captain,"

he urged, "what about one more shot at getting him to hold off—at least until the light's better and he's had——"

"The decision's been made," said Treleaven curtly. "The guy's nervy enough. If we argue with him now, he's finished." Burdick shrugged and turned away. Treleaven continued in a quieter tone, "I understand your feelings, Harry. But understand his too, surrounded by a mass of hardware he's never seen before. He's on a razor edge."

"What if he comes in badly?" put in Grimsell. "What's your plan?"

"He probably will, let's face it," Treleaven retorted grimly. "If it's hopeless, I'll try to bring him round again. We'll save any further arguments on the air unless it's obvious he doesn't stand a chance. Then I'll try to insist he puts down in the ocean." He listened for a moment to the calm recital of radar readings in his earphones, then pressed the switch of the microphone. "George. Let your air speed come back to 160 knots and hold it steady there."

The amplifier came alive as 714 took the air. There was an agonizing pause before Janet's voice intoned, "We are still losing height. Over."

Like a huge and ponderous bird, the Empress moved slowly past the western end of the Landsdowne Race Track, hidden now in the early-morning mist, and over the arm of the Fraser River. To the right the bridge from the mainland to Sea Island was just discernible.

"Good," said Treleaven. "Now set your mixture controls to take-off—that is, up to the top position." He fixed his eyes on his wrist watch, counting the sweep of the second hand. "Take your time,

George. When you're ready, turn your carburetor heat controls to cold. They're just forward of the throttles."

"How about the gas tanks?" Burdick demanded hoarsely.

"We checked earlier," replied Grimsell. "He's on main wing tanks now."

In the aircraft Spencer peered apprehensively from one control to the next. His face was a rigid mask. He heard Treleaven's voice resume its inexorable monologue. "The next thing, George, is to set the air filter to ram and the supercharges to low. Take your time, now." Spencer looked about him wildly. "The air filter control is the single lever below the mixture controls. Move it into the up position."

"Can you see it, Janet?" asked Spencer anxiously.

"Yes. Yes, I have it." She added quickly, "Look— the airport's right below us! You can see the long main runway."

"*Plenty* long, I hope," Spencer gritted, not lifting his head.

"The supercharger controls," continued Treleaven, "are four levers to the right of the mixture controls. Move them to the up position also."

"Got them?" said Spencer.

"Yes."

"Good girl." He was conscious of the horizon line dipping and rising in front of him, but dared not release his eyes from the panel. The roar of the engines took on a fluctuating tone.

"Now let's have that 15 degrees of flap." Treleaven instructed, "15 degrees—down to the second notch. The indicator dial is in the center of the main panel. When you have 15 degrees on, bring your air speed back slowly to 140 knots and adjust your trim for level flight. As soon as you've done that, switch the hydraulic booster pump on—extreme left, by the gyro control."

Through Treleaven's headset, the radar operator interposed, "Turn on to 225. I'm getting a height reading, Captain. He's all over the place. Nine hundred, up to thirteen hundred feet."

"Change course to 225," said Treleaven. "And watch your height—it's too irregular. Try to keep steady at 1,000 feet."

"He's dropping off fast," said the operator. "1,-000 ... 1,000 ... 900 ... 800 ... 700...."

"Watch your height!" Treleaven warned. "Use more throttle! Keep the nose up!"

"650 ... 600 ... 550...."

"Get back that height!" barked Treleaven. "Get it back! You need a thousand feet."

"550 ... 450 ..." called off the operator, calm but sweating. "This isn't good, Captain. 400 ... 400 ... 450—he's going up. 500...."

For a moment, Treleaven cracked. He tore off his headset and swung round to Burdick. "He can't fly it!" he shouted. "Of course he can't fly it!"

"Keep talking to him!" Burdick spat out, lunging forward at the captain and seizing his arm. "Keep talking, for Christ's sake. Tell him what to do."

Treleaven grabbed at the microphone, bringing it to his mouth. "Spencer," he said urgently, "you can't come straight in! Listen to me. You've *got* to do some circuits and practice that approach. There's enough fuel left for two hours' flying. Stay up, man! Stay up!"

They listened intently as Spencer's voice came through.

"You'd better get this, down there. I'm coming in. Do you hear me? *I'm coming in.* There are people up here who'll die in less than an hour, never mind two. I may bend the airplane a bit—that's a chance we have to take. Now get on with the landing check. I'm putting the gear down now." They heard him say, "Wheels down, Janet."

"All right, George, all right," said Treleaven heavily. He slipped the headset on again. He had recovered his composure, but a muscle in his jaw worked convulsively. He closed his eyes for a second, then opened them, speaking with his former crispness. "If your undercarriage is down, check for the three green lights, remember? Keep your heading steady on 225. Increase your throttle setting slightly to hold your air speed now the wheels are down. Adjust your trim and keep all the height you can. Right. Check that the brake pressure is showing around 1,000 pounds—the gauge is to the right of the hydraulic booster on the panel. If the pressure's okay, don't answer. You with me? Then open the gills to one third. D'you remember, Janet? The switch is by your left knee and it's marked in thirds. Answer me only if I'm going too fast. Next, the intercoolers. . . ."

As Treleaven went on, his voice filling the hushed control tower, Burdick moved to the plate glass window, searching the sky low on the horizon. The dawn light was murky, retarded by thick cloud banks. He heard Treleaven instruct a gentle 180-degree turn to the left, to bring the aircraft back for its last approach, impressing on Spencer to take it slowly and easily while the last checks

158

were carried out. The captain's precise monotone formed a somber background to the thoughts of the frantically worried airline manager.

"This," he said to an operator sitting nearby, "is a real tight one." The operator grimaced. "One thing's for sure," said Burdick. "Whatever happens in the next two or three minutes, there'll be hell let loose around here." He patted his trousers for cigarettes, thought better of it, and wiped the back of his hand across his mouth.

"Now advance your propeller settings," Treleaven was saying, "so that the tachometers give a reading of twenty-two fifty r.p.m. on each engine. Don't acknowledge."

"Twenty-two fifty," Spencer repeated to himself, watching the dials closely as he made the adjustment. "Janet," he said, "Let me hear the air speed."

"It's 130 ..." she began tonelessly, "125 ... 120 ... 125 ... 130...."

In the control tower Treleaven listened on his headphones to the steady voice from the radar room. "Height is still unsteady. Nine hundred feet."

"George," said Treleaven, "let your air speed come back to 120 knots and adjust your trim. I'll repeat that. Air speed 120." He looked down at his watch. "Take it nice and easy, now."

"Still losing height," reported the radar operator. "800 feet ... 750 ... 700...."

"You're losing height!" rapped out Treleaven. "You're losing height. Open up—open up! You must keep at around one thousand."

Janet continued her reading of the air speed:

"110 . . . 110 . . . 105 . . . 110 . . . 110 . . . 120 . . . 120 . . . 120. . . . steady at 120. . . ."

"Come up . . . come up!" gritted Spencer between his teeth, hauling on the control column. "What a lumbering, great wagon this is! It doesn't respond! It doesn't respond at all."

"125 . . . 130 . . . 130 . . . steady on 130. . . ."

"Height coming up to 900 feet," intoned the radar operator. "950 . . . on 1,000 now. Maintain 1,000."

Treleaven called to the tower controller, "He's turning on to final. Put out your runway lights, except zero-eight." He spoke into the microphone. "Straighten out on a heading between 074 and 080. Watch your air speed and your height. Keep at a thousand feet until I tell you."

In one series after another, the strings of lights half-sunken into the grass beside the runways flicked off, leaving just one line on either side of the main landing strip.

"Come out of your turn, George, when you're ready," said Treleaven, "and line up with the runway you'll see directly ahead of you. It's raining, so you'll want your windshield wipers. The switch is down at the right on the copilot's side and is clearly marked."

"Find it, Janet," said Spencer.

"Hold your height at a thousand feet, George. We've taken you a long way out, so you have lots of time. Have Janet look for the landing light switch. It's in the panel overhead, a little left of center. Hold your height steady."

"Can you find the switch?" asked Spencer.

"Just a minute . . . yes, I've got it."

Spencer stole a quick look ahead. "My God," he

breathed. The lights of the runway, brilliant pinpoints in the blue-gray overcast of dawn, seemed at this distance to be incredibly narrow, like a short section of railway track. He freed one hand for an instant to dash it across his eyes, watering from their concentration.

"Correct your course," said Treleaven. "Line yourself up straight and true. Hold that height, George. Now listen carefully. Aim to touch down about a third of the way along the runway. There's a slight cross wind from the left, so be ready with gentle right rudder." Spencer brought the nose slowly round. "If you land too fast, use the emergency brakes. You can work them by pulling the red handle immediately in front of you. And if that doesn't stop you, cut the four ignition switches which are over your head."

"See those switches, Janet?"

"Yes."

"If I want them off it'll be in a hurry," said Spencer. "So if I shout, don't lose any time about it." His throat was parched; it felt full of grit.

"All right," Janet replied in a whisper. She clasped her hands together to stop them shaking.

"It won't be long now, anyway. What about the emergency bell?"

"I hadn't forgotten. I'll ring it just before touchdown."

"Watch that air speed. Call it off."

"120 . . . 115 . . . 120. . . ."

"Begin descent," said the radar operator. "400 feet a minute. Check landing gear and flaps. Hold present heading."

"All right, George," said Treleaven, "put down full flap. Bring your air speed back to 115, adjust

161

your trim, and start losing height at 400 feet a minute. I'll repeat that. Full flap, air speed 115, let down at 400 feet a minute. Hold your present heading." He turned to Grimsell. "Is everything ready on the field?"

The controller nodded. "As ready as we'll ever be."

"Then this is it. In sixty seconds we'll know."

They listened to the approaching whine of engines. Treleaven reached out and took a pair of binoculars the controller handed him.

"Janet, give me full flap!" ordered Spencer. She thrust the lever down all the way. "Height and air speed—call them off!"

"1,000 feet . . . speed 130 . . . 800 feet, speed 120 . . . 700 feet, speed 105. We're going down too quickly!"

"Get back that height!" Treleaven shouted. "Get back! You're losing height too fast."

"I know, I know!" Spencer shouted back. He pushed the throttles forward. "Keep watching it!" he told the girl.

"650 feet, speed 100 . . . 400 feet, speed 100. . . ."

Eyes smarting with sweat in his almost feverish concentration, he juggled to correlate speed with an even path of descent, conscious with a deep, sickening terror of the relentless approach of the runway, nearer with every second. The aircraft swayed from side to side, engines alternately revving and falling.

Burdick yelled from the tower balcony, "Look at him! He's got no control!"

Keeping his glasses leveled at the oncoming aircraft, Treleaven snapped into the microphone, "Open up! Open up! You're losing height too fast!

Watch the air speed, for God's sake. Your nose is too high—open up quickly or she'll stall! Open up, I tell you, *open up!*"

"He's heard you," said Grimsell. "He's recovering."

"Me too, I wish," said Burdick.

The radar operator announced, "Still 100 feet below glide path. 50 feet below glide path."

"Get up—up," urged Treleaven. "If you haven't rung the alarm bell yet, do it now. Seats upright, passengers' heads down."

As the shrill warning rang out in the aircraft, Baird roared at the top of his voice, "Everybody down! Hold as tight as you can!"

Crouched double in their seats, Joe and Hazel Greer, the sports fans, wrapped their arms round each other, quietly and composedly. Moving clumsily in his haste, Childer tried to gather his motionless wife to him, then hurriedly leaned himself across her as far as he could. From somewhere midship came the sob-racked sound of a prayer and, further back, an exclamation from one of the rye-drinking quartet of, "God help us—this is it!"

"Shut up!" rapped 'Otpot. "Save your breath!"

In the tower, Grimsell spoke into a telephone-type microphone. "All fire-fighting and salvage equipment stand fast until the aircraft has passed them. She may swing." His voice echoed back metallically from the buildings.

"He's back up to 200 feet," reported radar. "Still below glide path. 150 feet. Still below glide path. He's too low, Captain. 100 feet.

Treleaven dragged off the headset. He jumped to his feet, holding the microphone in one hand and the binoculars in the other.

163

"Maintain that height," he instructed, "until you get closer in to the runway. Be ready to ease off gently.... Let down again.... That looks about right...."

"Damn the rain," cursed Spencer. "I can hardly see." He could make out that they were over grass. Ahead he had a blurred impression of the beginning of the runway.

"Watch the air speed," cautioned Treleaven. "Your nose is creeping up." There was a momentary sound of other voices in the background. "Straighten up just before you touch down and be ready to meet the drift with right rudder.... All right... Get ready to round out...."

The end of the gray runway, two hundred feet across, slid under them.

"Now!" Treleaven exclaimed. "You're coming in too fast. Lift the nose up! Get it up! Back up the throttles—right back! Hold her off. Not too much—not too much! Be ready for that cross wind. Ease her down, now. Ease her down!"

Undercarriage within a few feet of the runway surface, Spencer moved the control column gently back and forth, trying to feel his way down on to the ground, his throat constricted with panic because he now realized how much higher was this cockpit than that of any other plane he had flown, making judgment almost impossible for him.

For what seemed an age, the wheels skimmed the runway, making no contact. Then with a jolt they touched down. There was a shriek of rubber and a puff of smoke. The shock bounced the aircraft right into the air again. Then the big tires were once more fighting to find a purchase on the concrete.

A third bump followed, then another and yet another. Cursing through his clenched teeth, Spencer hauled the control column back into his stomach, all the nightmare fears of the past few hours now a paralyzing reality. The gray stream below him jumped up, receded jumped up again. Then, miraculously, it remained still. They were down. He eased on the toe brakes, then held them hard, using all the strength in his legs. There was a high-pitched squeal but no sudden drop in speed. From the corner of his eye he could see that they were already more than two thirds down the length of the runway. He could never hold the aircraft in time.

"You're landing too fast," roared Treleaven. "Use the emergency brakes! Pull the red handle!"

Spencer tugged desperately on the handle. He hauled the control column back into his stomach, jammed his feet on the brakes. He felt the tearing strain in his arms as the aircraft tried to slew. The wheels locked, skidded, then ran free again.

"Cut the switches!" he shouted. With a sweep of her hand Janet snapped them off. The din of the engines died away, leaving in the cabin the hum of gyros and radio equipment, and outside the screaming of tires.

Spencer stared ahead in fascinated horror. With no sound of engines, the aircraft was still traveling fast, the ground leaping past them in a blur. He could see now a big checkerboard marking the turn at the far end of the runway. In the fraction of a second his eyes registered the picture of a fire truck, its driver falling to the ground in his scramble to get away.

165

Treleaven's voice burst into his ears with the force of a blow.

"Ground-loop it to the left! Ground-loop it to the left! Hard left rudder!"

Making an instantaneous decision, Spencer put his left foot on the rudder pedal and threw all his weight behind it, pressing it forward savagely.

Veering suddenly from the runway, the aircraft began to swing in an arc. Flung over to the right side of his seat, Spencer struggled to keep the wings clear of the ground. There was a rending volume of noise, a dazzling flash, as the undercarriage ripped away and the aircraft smashed to the ground on its belly. The impact lifted Spencer clean from his seat. He felt a sharp pain as his safety belt bit deeply into his flesh.

"Get your head down!" he yelled. "We're piling up!"

Gripping their seats against the maniacal violence of the bouncing and rocking, they tried to curl themselves up. Still under momentum, the aircraft continued to slither crabwise, ploughing the grass in vicious furrows. With a screech of metal it crossed another runway, uprooting the runway lights, showering fountains of earth up into the air.

Spencer prayed for the end.

Like a prisoner in some crazy, helpless juggernaut, blood appearing in the corner of his mouth from a chance blow as yet unfelt, he waited for the inevitable tip-over, the upending, splintering crash that would, for him, disintegrate into a thousand fiery pinpoints of light before they were swallowed into darkness.

Then, quite suddenly, they were moving no longer. Spencer seemed to feel the same crazy motions as if they were still careering across the field; but, his eyes told him they had stopped. For the space of seconds there was no sound at all. He braced himself against the awkward sideways tilt of the deck and looked over at Janet. Her head was buried in her hands. She was crying silently.

In the passenger compartment behind him there were murmurs and rustlings as of people who unbelievably awake to find themselves still alive. Someone laughed, shortly and hysterically, and this seemed to let loose half a dozen voices speaking at once.

He heard Baird call out, "Is anyone hurt?"

The noises melted into confusion. Spencer closed his eyes. He felt himself shaking.

"Better open up the emergency doors," came the adenoidal tones of 'Otpot, "and then everyone stay where he is."

From the door to the flight deck, jammed open in the crash, he heard the doctor exclaim, "Wonderful job! Spencer! Are you both all right?"

"I ground-looped!" he muttered to himself in disgust. "We turned right around the way we came. What a performance—to ground-loop!"

"Rubbish—you did magnificently," Baird retorted. "As far as I can tell, there are only bruises and a bit of shock back here. Let's have a look at the captain and first officer—they must have been thrown about some."

Spencer turned to him. It was painful to move his neck.

"Doctor"—his throat was hoarse—"are we in time?"

"Yes, just about, I'd say. It's up to the hospital now, anyway. You've done your part."

He tried to raise himself in his seat. At that moment he became aware of the sound of crackling. He felt an upsurge of alarm. Then he realized that the noise was issuing from his head set which had slipped to the deck. He reached down and picked it up, holding one phone to his ear.

"George Spencer!" Treleaven was calling. "George Spencer! Are you there?"

Outside there was now a rising crescendo of sirens from crash tenders and fire trucks and ambulances. Spencer heard voices in the passenger compartment behind him.

"Yes," he said, "I'm here."

Treleaven was jubilant, caught in the general reaction. Behind his voice there were sounds of excited conversation and laughter.

"George. That was probably the lousiest landing in the history of this airport. So don't ever ask us for a job as a pilot. But there are some of us here who'd like to shake your hand, and later we'll buy you a drink. Now hold everything, George. We're coming over."

Janet had raised her head and was smiling tremulously.

"You should see your face," she said. "It's black."

He couldn't think of a thing to say. No witticism; no adequate word of thanks. He knew only that he was intolerably tired and sick to the stomach. He reached over for her hand and grinned back.